# Wicked
## REUNION

## ALSO BY MICHELLE A. VALENTINE

**The Black Falcon Series**

*Rock the Beginning*

*Rock the Heart*

*Rock the Band*

*Rock My Bed*

*Rock My World*

*Rock the Beat*

*Rock My Body*

**Hard Knocks Series**

*Phenomenal X*

Coming Soon: *Xavier Cold*

**The Collectors Series**

*Demon at My Door*

Coming Soon: *Demon in My Bed*

**A Sexy Manhattan Fairytale Series**

*Naughty King*

*Feisty Princess*

Coming Soon: *Dirty Royals*

**Wicked White Series**

*Wicked White*

# Wicked REUNION

## A WICKED WHITE NOVEL

MICHELLE A. VALENTINE

Montlake
Romance

Text copyright © 2015 Michelle A. Valentine
All rights reserved.

Published by Montlake Romance, Seattle

www.apub.com

Amazon, the Amazon logo, and Montlake Romance are trademarks of Amazon.com, Inc., or its affiliates.

ISBN-13: 9781503949959
ISBN-10: 1503949958

Cover design by Letitia Hasser

Printed in the United States of America

*To all of our service members and their families,*
*thank you*

## THEN
## LONDON

The energy on the field is electric. Everyone in the stadium is on their feet, cheering as loud as they can while they wait for their team to rush onto the dark-green grass. The love of baseball is one of the things that drew my boyfriend, Jared, and me together in the first place. I love the sport, and he always excelled at it. Playing college ball is a dream come true for him, and I couldn't be more proud of him if I tried.

"Now introducing your Tennessee Volunteers. The junior pitcher, number twenty-three, Jared Kraft!" the announcer calls overhead, and the crowd immediately goes wild.

Jared runs out into the middle of the stadium in his orange-and-white uniform. Instantly my heart swells with pride for the man I love.

Sam nudges my shoulder with hers as she continues to shake her pom-poms in time with mine to match the beat of the music playing overhead. "Gah! London, do you hear this crowd? The way these people go nuts for him makes you think Jared's already playing pro ball."

I laugh as we watch all the action taking place on the field from our seats right behind the dugout. "That is the plan, you know. Jared may skip his senior year of college and go right into the draft. The coaches think he'll be ready after this season."

Sam's green eyes widen. "Really? Aren't you worried?"

"About what?" I ask as the rest of the players continue to run out from the tunnel leading from the locker room.

"The long-distance thing—doesn't that scare you? Guys seem to lose their ever-lovin' minds once big money starts rolling in. If you're still here, London, you won't be around to put the brakes on Jared or keep the gold diggers away from him."

I shrug. Her words, no matter how true they may be in most cases, don't worry me a bit. Jared and I are too strong to be broken apart over something so trivial as distance. "We're a package deal. We've been attached at the hip since we were in middle school, so I don't worry about that with us. Besides, wherever he goes, I'll just transfer to a school in that city and finish up my degree."

Sam's face twists like she's just sucked on a lemon. "You'll give up everything—your entire life here, including your dad—just like that for him?"

I nod as my gaze shoots to the middle of the field, where I spot Jared standing proudly with his team, and I answer her question with ease. "Love requires sacrifice sometimes."

She shakes her head, causing her blond ponytail to swish back and forth while she laughs. "Girl, you've got it bad. I hope that guy appreciates what he's got with you. Not many girls would give up everything for a man."

I sigh as my thoughts drift to just how much Jared means to me and what I would do in order to stay with him. He was there for me when my mom passed away when I was just a kid. Even at twelve years old, he knew just what to say in order to help my heart heal. I'll always love him for that, and there's nothing I wouldn't do for him. "They would if they experienced a love like the one I've got."

Almost as if on cue, Jared looks in my direction and winks as he stands with his team. I smile because I know that I mean just as much to him as he does to me. Nothing will ever come between us.

Nothing.

## 2

### *NOW*
### JARED

**M**y fingers fly over the frets as my other hand stays busy picking the strings to get the notes just right. The chords sound amazing, and I know once the label realizes how well I can shred, they'll give me a chance to jump on the mic and lay down some vocals too. Our band's manager knows how well I can sing.

"No. No. No. That's not the way it's written, JJ." Ace's voice cuts through my euphoric music high and grounds me instantly.

This douche is about to get on my last fucking nerve.

I take a deep breath and force myself to stay seated in this studio chair and not rage out like I want to. "What now? That's exactly how it's written, and I was playing the shit out of it too before you stopped me. Why don't you head back into the booth and let the producer do his fucking job? If I wasn't doing it to his liking, he would've spoken up. I don't need your two cents on everything I do. I was hired because I'm damn good at what I do, so don't treat me like a moron."

The muscles in my back tense as I stare into Ace's brown eyes. I have to force myself to hold back from telling him off like I want. Everyone treats this guy like he's gold—like he's some fucking golden child who can do no wrong—and it pisses me off. I'm just as good as him. I don't see where he gets off with this attitude that he's my boss. That motherfucker has another thing coming if he thinks for one damn minute that he's better than me.

Ace's nostrils flare and I can tell I'm getting to him.

Good.

I want the fucker to quit.

We've never hit it off. If it hadn't been for the studio putting us in a band together under contract, there would be no way I would work with this guy. He's a condescending asshole who thinks he's so smart. I would quit myself, except the pay is exceptional and music is the one thing in my life that I'm still very passionate about. Music is the one thing I know I'm damn good at. Besides, I'm not really qualified to do much of anything else. These days it seems like you need a college degree to land a good job, and since I don't have one of those, I'm smart enough to stay put and put up with Ace's bullshit. I mean, there's always at least one person that you hate at any job, right?

Ace pinches the bridge of his nose and tips his head down, causing his long bronze hair to fall like a curtain around his face. It's like he has to take a second to calm down before addressing me. We've known each other a little over two years, but in that time I've learned that, like me, Ace is a hothead, and the two of us together don't mesh well.

When Ace's gaze shifts back to me, he runs his hand over his face and smooths down his long beard. "Look, I know I can be a little overbearing when it comes to music, but I just want it to be perfect. I don't mean to be a complete dick when I call things out like that. I just get so passionate that I can't contain myself. I know you're good. Anyone can see that, so I'll try to back off a bit."

I raise my eyebrows. While that's not exactly an apology, it's the closest thing I've ever gotten from him, and the last thing I ever expected.

Apologies aren't easy. God, I know that more than anyone, because there are people in my life who deserve one from me who've never gotten it and probably never will. I mean, how can you possibly say sorry for ruining someone's life?

My mind instantly drifts off to the last time I saw London and the things I said to her. So many times I've wanted to pick up the phone just to hear her voice and beg her to forgive me, but I know it's too late now. Too much time has passed between us, and I'm sure she's moved on by now. London is one piece of my past I have to continue locking away. It hurts me too much to think about her.

I clear my throat. "Whatever, man. I'll play it again as long as you go back to the booth. I don't want you in here breathing down my neck."

Ace holds up his hands and nods. "Fair enough."

Without any additional argument, he turns around and heads back into the sound booth. When I'm alone again in the room, the producer gives me the go sign to start from the top of the song. I take a deep breath, close my eyes, and allow my fingers to find the chords. This time I make it all the way through without one interruption, and I don't mean to brag, but it was damn near perfect.

"That sounded great, JJ. You're wrapped," the producer says into my headphones and then gives me a thumbs-up when my eyes flick in his direction.

Instantly I pull the headphones off and toss them aside before I unplug my guitar and place it back inside the case. Just as I snap the last latch closed and stand, the door to the recording booth opens.

Jane Ann, the band's tour manager, stands there in the doorway, wearing one of her signature all-red outfits that match her flaming hair perfectly. Her arms are folded tightly against her chest, and there's a hideous scowl on her face, pointed in my direction.

Fuck. She's pissed, and I can probably guess what this is all about.

My shoulders sag. Not this shit again. I'm so not in the mood. "What?"

She arches one of her perfectly plucked red eyebrows at me. "Don't play dumb with me. I know you better than that, JJ. You are too smart to not know why I'm pissed right now."

I roll my eyes as I push past her with my guitar case in hand. I'm not doing this in here with an audience on the other side of that glass—I'm sick of having this conversation, period.

Jane Ann doesn't take the hint, because she's hot on my heels as I make my way out of the studio and down the hallway. "JJ!"

The way she calls my stage name makes me cringe, and I wish that I could reply with a big "fuck off." I hate that this woman has so much power over me—and the band, for that matter—but the reality of the situation is this woman is my boss.

"Why do you have to defend him, Jane Ann?" I call over my shoulder to her as I keep walking. "He's not that fucking great."

I finally come to the exit and spot the beat-up, blue F-250 pickup truck that's belonged to me since college and keep trudging toward it.

Jane Ann doesn't take the hint, though, because she remains right on my heels through the parking lot. The woman is relentless.

"Not that great? You are joking, right? Ace White is the entire reason Wicked White has had the level of success it's achieved on the first record." There's a bit of a growl in her voice. I can tell that she doesn't like that I've just insulted her so-called top musical find.

I release a sarcastic laugh. "That's fucking rich. Have you forgotten that it takes all four of us to make this band happen? Without Tyler, Luke, and me, there would be no Wicked White. Ace is just the face *you* all chose to promote."

I unlock the truck and jerk open the driver's-side door. If I didn't love my guitar, I'd be tempted to throw it inside versus sliding it gently behind the seat.

"We're not on this again, are we?" The annoyance in her voice is unmistakable as she refers to the one thing she knows I deserve.

I spin around. "You're damn straight we are. I don't know why it's so hard to give me the opportunity that *you* promised me when I signed my contract. It was supposed to be me singing on those tracks. I'm not just some guitarist—"

She narrows her eyes and cuts me off. "That's exactly what *you* are. I found you playing in some dive with a band that was going nowhere. When I offered you a spot in the band that Mopar Records was building, you were eager to sign my deal because you knew you'd never get this far on your own."

"I would've—"

A bitter laugh comes out of her mouth. "No. Don't kid yourself, sweetie. Without me you'd still be in that bar band, living out of your truck. You should be thankful that I picked you and turned you into JJ White—Jared Kraft was going nowhere—but it seems to me that you're ungrateful for the setup you've been given. I could fire you anytime I want and have you replaced the same day. Don't forget that."

I flinch like she's just smacked me in the face. "You really think I'm *that* replaceable? I'd like to see you try to find someone else who would be willing to put up with your shit, and don't even get me started on how big of a pain in the ass Ace is."

Jane Ann points her finger at me. "Don't push me, JJ." She closes her index finger and thumb together, leaving less than a half inch of space between them. "I'm this close to canning your ass. If you weren't so ridiculously good-looking, I already would have. You're lucky the girls like you. This whole rebel-without-a-cause thing you've got going on is your saving grace because it works for your moody ass, but I swear that I'll find another pretty face to replace you if you don't find some common ground and quit fighting with Ace every chance you get. Get your shit together. I mean it. This is your last warning."

I open my mouth to tell her to fuck off, but the expression on her face is daring me to, because she's looking for a reason to get rid of me. We've never really seen eye to eye since she brought Ace on board. I never trusted her after that.

Most people would think I'm nuts for staying in a band I hate so much.

Truth is? I love music, and I'll do anything to be able to keep it in my life. It's the only thing I've got left.

## 3

*NOW*
## LONDON

I sit on the funky floral-pattern chair in our bedroom and rub my fingers over the coarse material on the armrest to distract myself from the scene before me. It's not one that I'm ready to deal with, but deep down I know it needs to happen.

Wes carefully folds the last few of his T-shirts and puts them in his suitcase. The sound of the zipper locking his stuff inside is so loud in the otherwise-silent room that it causes my breath to catch.

His brown eyes flick to mine, and it saddens me to know this is probably the last time I'll be in a bedroom with my husband. He's handsome, and he turns women's heads everywhere we go with his toned body, sandy-blond hair, and deep, soulful brown eyes. On top of all that, he's brilliant too—one of the brightest young engineers at his firm. He's the complete package, but he's not Jared—the one man that I can't seem to get over—and Wes knows it. It's the reason we've struggled over the past three months of our short marriage. Wes is just too big of a reminder of what I've lost, and no matter how hard I try, I just can't seem to get over the past and move forward.

I tried to break free of the memory of Jared the best way I knew how: by dating other men. It never worked. All I ended up doing was comparing every guy to Jared, including Wes.

Wes understood my heartbreak—he'd witnessed every facet of my relationship with Jared—and was patient with me, even willing to put up with my obsession with a man who no longer wanted me.

Wes has really been a good friend, and I love him for that, but unfortunately, that's all I still see him as—a friend. He provided a distraction to the real issues I was struggling with—the grief and depression that accompany a broken heart.

The thought of smothering all the memories I have of Jared sounded amazing. I was so tired of hurting and longing for a relationship that I knew was well over that I allowed myself to get lost in Wes for a while. It's clear that Wes loves me, and I really thought that eventually his love would make me forget my past and help me move on. But it didn't work.

I'm so stupid to hang on to a memory of a man who is nothing more than a ghost to everyone who once knew him.

Wes shoves his hands deep in his pockets and his shoulders slump forward. "I think I've got all my personal stuff. If I've left anything else, just box it up for me, and I'll pick it up at some point."

I nod, fighting back the tears. "Okay."

Wes bites his bottom lip as he walks around to sit on the end of the bed across from me. He reaches out and places his hand gently on my left knee. "It's going to be okay, London. Things between us just didn't work. We moved way too fast, and I'm willing to give you all the time you need to work through this—to see that you made the right choice by being with me—because I love you. I won't lie and say that this doesn't tear me up inside, but I understand why you couldn't give me all your heart, because it still belongs to someone else. It sucks, but I'll just have to get over it and hope that we can find a way to be together."

His kind words remind me of why I fell for him and only make me cry harder. I cover my face with my hands. "I'm so sorry, Wes. I didn't mean for this to happen. I'm an awful human being."

Wes leans in and wraps his arms around me, allowing the sweet scent of his cologne to envelop me. "Shhh. Don't say that. You can't help who you love or what your heart chooses to hold on to. Who knows? Maybe when you're ready, we can try this again."

I cling to him as I cry because I know how much I've hurt him. I don't deserve his kindness, I know that, but I'm grateful for it.

He holds me against him and allows me to get everything out of my system, and once I'm able to pull myself together from hysterically sobbing, he leans back so he can stare into my eyes. "Are you going to be all right by yourself tonight? I can call someone. My mom—Sam, maybe?"

I shake my head. "She's got her hands full with Brody, and I don't want to bog her down even more with my issues. Your mother—I can't even fathom facing her right now. She'll hate me for this."

"No, she won't. Mom loves you." He reaches toward my face but then stops himself from touching my cheek before sighing heavily. "I wish you would've let me in. All I've ever wanted to do is love you, and for you to love me back."

I bite my bottom lip, and it takes every inch of my willpower to not burst into tears again. I can't respond. If I open my mouth to answer that, I won't be able to pretend that I'm keeping it all together, because I'm an absolute, confused mess.

If I could let Wes in, things in my life would be so much easier, but I just can't. I should've realized from the start that loving him would be impossible.

Wes pushes himself up and stands before me, a frown etched on his face. "I feel terrible leaving you like this. It's hard for me to watch you cry. I've never been able to take seeing you sad."

I sniff, not wanting to burden him any more than I already have. I want him to be able to walk out the door without a guilty conscience, because this is my fault—my problem—not his. "I'll be okay. I promise."

Wes sighs again, like it's the only thing he can do, because his heart is so heavy, and awkwardness eats up every inch of the room. It's hard to tell someone who you love that you're not in love with them—at least not in the way they want you to love them. If I'm being honest, I'm not really sure I ever loved Wes as anything more than a friend, and that makes me a horribly selfish person. It's so hard to push away such a nice guy, but I know he deserves better than what I've been giving him in this marriage. He deserves to be loved in a way that I'm not capable of.

The moment Wes steps around the side of the bed and grabs the handle of the suitcase, he glances back at me as if to give me one more chance to stop him from walking out my door and changing the dynamic between us forever, but I remain still as stone in my seat.

My lips pull in a tight line, and the skin on the bridge of my nose pinches together as I wrinkle my face and refuse to allow any emotion to escape and expose how torn up I am. Wes frowns when he realizes that I'm not going to beg him to stay, and he picks up the bag and walks out of the room.

The moment the front door closes, I release the sob I kept stuffed down in my chest. Instantly I know the security bubble that Wes created for me, the one that masked all the pain I've been dealing with for the past five years, is gone for good.

## 4

### *THEN*
### JARED

The wind whips through my hair as I drive down Main Street at one in the morning. I stick my hand out the open window, allowing the cool night air to flow through my fingers. Things couldn't be more perfect. Everything in my life is lining up, and it feels amazing.

Most people say I live a blessed life, and I can't argue otherwise. I'm starting pitcher at the University of Tennessee in my hometown of Knoxville, I have a damn near perfect family, and most importantly, the most beautiful girl I've ever seen belongs to me. When you consider my personal life, and add in the fact that my team has just won their fourth straight game and the pro scouts are swarming around me like crazy, I don't think a luckier man has ever walked this earth. I've got everything going for me.

I glance down at London, who is curled up on the bench seat next to me in the truck. Her pouty pink lips are partially open, and her eyelids are closed over her green eyes. Soft brown curls cascade around me, tickling my arm as she rests her head on my shoulder.

The rhythmic rise and fall of her chest tells me that she's fast asleep. I love that she's so comfortable with me, knowing that I'll always be there, protecting her, just like I have been since we were kids. The fruity scent of her shampoo mixed with her perfume comforts me as I drive us home. London has been the one constant in my life since she saw me and my brother playing ball in the middle of the street and demanded that we let her play. Even though we were only in middle school, it didn't take long for me to fall in love with the cute brunette girl who loved baseball as much as me. Next to London, the only other people that matter to me are my mom and dad, along with my brother, Wes. Those four mean everything to me.

I turn into the subdivision that London and I grew up in. It's nothing extravagant. Older, split-level homes built in the early eighties line the streets, and the moment I turn down our street, a warm feeling of ease comes over me. This place—this town—fits us, and the thought of leaving here when I turn pro scares me a bit, but I know it's a place that I can always come back to. Besides, I'm sure anywhere with London will feel like home.

I pull up in front of London's little brown house, throw the transmission into park, and nudge her. "Wake up, sleepy. You're home."

She rolls her shoulders and stretches before snaking her arms around my neck, pressing her body against me. "I can't wait until we get our own place. I hate spending a night without you."

"Soon." I pull her in tighter against my body and kiss the tip of her nose. "We're almost done with school. Everything is falling into place with our plan, and we'll be on to phase two before you know it."

"Ah. Phase two. Remind me what that one is again?" She gives me a mischievous grin, knowing exactly what it is. London loves making me repeat it to her every chance she gets.

"Let's see . . ." I drift off, playing along. "I think phase two involved getting a dog."

"Right after . . ." she prompts and raises her eyebrows expectantly.

"Right after—" I cut myself off, feeling for some reason it's the absolute perfect time to spring a surprise on her. I lean over and reach into the glove box of the truck and pull out a little black velvet box that I've been carrying around for over a week, waiting for just the right moment to ask London to make things very official with me.

London's green eyes widen at the sight of the little box that gives away the one question I want to ask her—the one question that will bond us together forever. Her lips gape open, and she instantly covers them with both hands.

"Jared? Oh my God. Is that? Are you . . . Is that what I think it is?" she asks behind muffling fingers, trying to hold in her excitement.

I laugh when I hear her use my real name, which she usually reserves for when I piss her off and she wants my full attention. This is obviously serious business.

I bite my bottom lip as I open the tiny box and show her the modest diamond ring inside. "It's not much, I know, and I want you to know that I plan on replacing it when I'm able."

She wraps her fingers around my wrists. "It's perfect. The ring doesn't matter. All that matters is that I have you."

"You'll always have me," I reply instantly, without another thought. My eyes flick down to her kissable mouth. I find myself unable to resist the temptation, so I lean in and press my lips against hers. She opens her mouth and admits my begging tongue. I cup her face and allow myself to revel in the moment before I pull back and stare deeply into her eyes. This woman is absolutely stunning, and I can't imagine that a more perfect person exists for me on this planet. "Will you marry me, London?"

She traces her fingers along my jawline, never breaking eye contact. "Of course I will."

"Yeah?" I laugh as I pull out the ring with shaky hands and then slide it onto her ring finger.

I don't ever remember feeling this happy and complete. Marrying London—officially making her mine—will be the best day of my life.

Her eyes brighten as a huge grin stretches across her face. "Was there ever any doubt? Marrying you has been my dream since I was twelve years old."

We both stare at the ring on her hand and all the promises to each other that it holds. I grasp her hand in mine and then kiss the ring as it sits on her finger. London might not realize it, but marrying her has been my dream for a very long time too. People always question me, especially other guys, on how I can be so sure that London is the right girl for me since she's the only one I've ever been with, and to that, my answer is simple: when you find your soul mate, you just know. Nothing else in the world matters but her, and no other woman on the planet can even compare.

This is right. Being with her is so easy, and I know it's the reason that I'm on this planet.

I cradle her face in my hands. "I love you, London. So much."

She blinks slowly, her incredibly long eyelashes fluttering as she smiles. "I love you too."

I lean in and press my lips to hers. The softness of her warm mouth against mine instantly turns me on, and a need to taste her pulses through me. I thread my fingers into her hair and flick my tongue against her lower lip, begging for entrance. When she obliges, I deepen our kiss and then grab her hips and hoist her onto my lap so she's straddling me with her back against the steering wheel.

My fingers dip under her T-shirt, and they trace the smooth skin just above the waistband of her jeans. This girl drives me out of my fucking mind with desire every time she comes within two feet of me. It doesn't matter that we've been together for years, because every time is just as exciting as the first. If anything, we get better every time we explore one another's bodies.

London rolls her hips against mine, and a moan slips out of her lips as she pushes herself against my hard cock inside my jeans. She always gets so turned on when she can feel how much I want her.

"Can we go somewhere?" she asks in a breathy voice as she continues to rock her hips and kiss me over and over.

As if of their own accord, my hands slide down her back and cup her ass. "Where do you have in mind?"

"Anywhere," she answers. "I just need to be with you."

Who am I to argue with a beautiful woman who is in desperate need of me?

The denim material of her shorts rides up her thighs, baring even more of her soft skin. My girl is fucking beautiful. Everything about her, I'm in love with it. Every move she makes turns me on, and I seize every opportunity I can to be inside her.

I cup her face in my hands and stare into her green eyes. "I love you, London."

"I love you too," she whispers back.

My fingers slide down her neck and across her exposed shoulders, only getting caught up a bit on her bra and tank top straps. I hook my index finger around the straps and slide them down, exposing the tops of her breasts. A pink, lacey bra covers her nipples, but my fingertips are able to trace the tops of the smooth, mounded flesh. My cock jerks inside my jeans, and if I don't have her soon, I might just fucking come in my pants.

London smiles because she can feel how turned on I am. She leans in and presses her lips to mine, allowing her dark hair to fall around us like a curtain. The sweet scent of her shampoo wafts around me, and I inhale it deeply.

I fucking love this woman so much that it physically hurts sometimes. There's nothing I wouldn't do for her, because she's my entire world.

I wrap my arms around her before crushing my lips to hers. Her mouth opens for me, and I plunge my tongue into her mouth. My hand runs up her back and then threads into her thick hair as she works her hips against me. A soft moan tells me that she's just as fucking turned on as I am.

"God, Jared. I want you." She tosses her head back and I drag my lips down her neck. "Right here. Right now."

That's the only thing she needs to say to have me revved up and ready to take her. I yank the buttons of her shorts open but leave her top on, because we're still parked on the street.

London rises up, making it easier for me to pull her shorts and panties off before I run my finger against her swollen clit. I work her into a frenzy and stare at her in awe as she leans back against the steering wheel to watch me pleasure her. The only thing that's rattling around in my brain is how I never want to lose this—how I always want London to be *mine*.

I slip my finger inside her. "So fucking wet. You are always so ready for me."

She bites her bottom lip. "That's because I always want you. Speaking of . . ."

London trails off as she quickly works at freeing my cock from my jeans, and once it springs free, she wraps her hand around the base and guides it into her entrance.

I fucking love when she takes control. Nothing is sexier than when she does that.

She drops her forehead down against mine and places a feather-light kiss on my lips.

Her wet tongue darts out from behind her teeth, and she licks her lips as she sits down and takes all of me inside her. My body shudders from pure delight when she quickens her pace of sliding up and down on my shaft. "Damn, you always feel so fucking amazing."

My fingers dig into her hips as I pump into her faster and harder, causing her let to out a moan.

"Oh, God. I'm coming," she cries out before she falls apart around me.

My mouth hangs open as I lock eyes with her, and warmth spreads over every inch of my body. I'm so close, but I don't want this to end so soon. Ever since we started fucking without condoms when she got on birth control, I can never last as long. The sensation of her wrapped around me just feels too fucking good.

I close my eyes and slip into sweet oblivion as I come hard inside the woman that I love.

After we're dressed, I pull London back into my lap and run my fingers through her soft brown curls. I can't wait until we have our own place someday and we can lie like this all night instead of hiding out in my truck to have sex.

A chill from the early spring air fills the cab, so I reach behind her and fumble around until I find the key to the ignition to get some heat going. But before I can crank the engine to life, a loud knock on the passenger-side window startles me.

London gasps and jerks her head toward the sound. "Shit. Jesus, Wes. You scared the hell out of me."

I laugh as she scolds my older brother and then crawls off my lap and over to the passenger side to crank open the window.

The moment London rolls the window all the way down, Wes leans into the cab of the truck with a wicked smile on his face. "You guys do realize that Old Man Jenkins is watching you, right? The two of you are giving him one hell of a show. This is the most action he's seen in a long time."

I glance over at the house across the street just in time to see the curtains shake as they're dropped back into place. "Dirty pervert needs to get laid, bad."

Wes nods in agreement, causing a strand of blond hair to flop over one eye. He quickly pushes it away. "He does, but until then I think he's going to continue watching every move London makes like a creeper, so I thought I'd give you guys a heads-up."

"Thanks, Wes," London says, and I notice her face is a deep shade of red. "I'm so mortified."

His eyes soften as he stares down at her. "No problem. Besides, don't sweat it too bad. I'm sure the old guy didn't see much."

My brow furrows the moment I catch my older brother staring at my girl just a few seconds too long for my comfort. When his eyes snap up in my direction, there's a flash of some unreadable emotion in them, but he quickly avoids my stare and shoves himself away from the truck.

"I'll see you around, London," he calls over his shoulder as he stalks off in the direction of our house, which is a block away.

I watch him walk down the sidewalk into the darkness of the night. Wes's hands are shoved deep in his pockets, and his shoulders slump inward, which in the past has always been a sure sign that he's uncomfortable. It's been his go-to move since we were kids, and I've seen it a million times, but for the life of me I can't figure out why he would be acting that way right now. Maybe he's embarrassed I just caught him looking at London, but it's not like it's the first time I've ever caught him doing that.

I'm pretty sure my brother has always had a thing for my girl, but he knows better than to ever act on it. For one, he knows that London is not interested, and two, he knows that just because he's a year older doesn't mean that I'm not capable of kicking his ass. All the time in the gym has served me well. Wes, while athletic, tends to spend most of his time nowadays studying. He's going to be an engineer, and his course load is crazy. He's definitely more of the brain in the family, where I am more of the brawn, but I'm not a dummy when it comes to books either. I just chose something a little easier as far as school goes. A business degree will serve me well when I'm negotiating deals when I go pro next year. I have the feeling I'll be reading over a lot of contracts.

"It was lucky Wes let us know about our audience. I was just about to rip off your clothes again and maul you here in the front seat in front of God and, well, everyone else who was watching," London teases and then sighs as she glances at the clock on the dashboard. "I should probably head in anyhow. It's late."

"Okay, babe. I'll see you tomorrow." I lean over and give her a quick kiss. "Do me a favor and keep the ring between you and me until I have a chance to tell Mom about it. I want to tell them both at the same time when Dad makes his weekly call home on Sunday."

London nods. "How's your dad doing over there? Did they say when he'll be able to come home yet? I know last time he called he was miserable with all the heat over there in Afghanistan."

"No, but he said they can't keep him over there much longer. His Stop Loss is about to be lifted, I think."

"That's the rule where they can keep someone in the service even after they've completed their time commitment to the military?"

I nod. "Yep. Things are looking better over there. After all, they've had nearly three years to get squared away since nine eleven. Dad told Mom that the most the army could hold them over there was two years solid without giving him time to come home, and we're coming up on the two-year mark in less than three months."

She reaches over and threads her fingers through mine, giving them a little squeeze. "I know how much you miss him. He'll be home soon."

I stare down at London's hand laced with mine, trying not to dwell on how much I actually miss my father. His Sunday-morning calls are the reason we come home every weekend instead of staying in our dorm rooms. I miss a lot of Sunday calls because I'm always traveling for away games with the team, but when I have home games, I'm here.

It's good to be able to hear his voice and know he's doing all right even though he's stuck in the middle of the desert, fighting for our country in what our government is calling Operation Iraqi Freedom. It's a war I only partially understand. I know there were a lot of lives lost when those planes hit our towers, and we need to retaliate and make sure that shit never happens on our soil again, but there're so many other political aspects that I don't get. Like why is my dad in Afghanistan if the people we're after are in Iraq? I just don't get it, and I sure as hell don't like it, because it's keeping Dad away from us.

Most people say that's what he signed up for when he joined the army. Maybe that's true of guys that enlist in active duty, but Dad is in the National Guard. The most he was ever gone when I was growing up was two weeks a year. I don't think he bargained for being away from his family for nearly two years.

London leans in and kisses my cheek, pulling me out of my thoughts. "I'll see you tomorrow."

She opens the passenger-side door and hops out.

"Good night, babe," I call to her before she shuts the door and heads up to her house.

If it weren't for London keeping my head on straight, I don't know what I would've done while Dad's been gone. It's like she's my guardian angel—one I'm glad to have in my life. I don't know what I'd ever do if I lost her.

## NOW
## LONDON

**B**right blue paint swirls onto the paper from my brush as all of the children lean over my shoulder. "You can use your imagination and make the house any color you want." I push the paint over the white paper with my brush as my preschool students watch while I quickly create a multicolored house in front of them. "Now, boys and girls, I want you to sit at your desk and paint a house, but make sure to keep it on the paper, please," I quickly add as they scamper off to their desks.

I walk from table to table along with my classroom assistant, Jenn, and make sure the children are all following directions. It's good to be here. It takes my mind off how absolutely quiet things are at home now that Wes is gone. I miss his companionship, but I know it's unfair of me to ask him to come back just because I'm lonely.

Peyton, the most inquisitive four-year-old I've ever met and the son of my longtime best friend, raises his hand. "Mrs. Kraft, can I make my house green?"

I smile. "Of course you can. It's your house. Any color you want, remember?"

Peyton's little strawberry-blond head instantly whips toward the little dark-haired girl, Brice, sitting beside him, and he fires an "I told you so" look at her before going back to work on the project before him.

I chuckle as I continue helping the children until it's time to clean up and get ready for their parents to come.

One by one my little distractions leave me to go on to their happy homes, until it's just Peyton and me left in the classroom. It's not unusual for him to be the last to be picked up. Sam always likes to hang out and chat with me a bit when she picks him up, so she always comes last so she's not monopolizing my time when the other parents come.

I pull out the tiny chair next to his and sit down beside Peyton while he plays with a superhero action figure, making it soar through the air, accompanied by matching sound effects.

"Who do you have here?" I ask, leaning over to get a better look at the red-caped crusader in his tiny hand.

"Superman!" he replies instantly with so much enthusiasm that it's infectious, causing me to smile.

"He's always been my favorite," I whisper like it's a big secret.

"Mine too," he answers and looks up at me with hazel eyes. "He reminds me of Daddy. The guys in the army call him Superman because he's so strong and can lift big weights."

The way he looks up to his dad, idolizing him, instantly reminds me of Jared and the way he was with his father. It's funny how the little things—something so minute—can spark a memory of someone you miss so much.

"I'm so sorry, London." My gaze snaps in the direction of the doorway as Sam walks through the door with a baby on her hip.

Her face is red—a stark contrast to her pale blond hair—and the expression on her face tells me she's stressed to no end. I feel for her because I don't know how she manages to keep things together, being on her own with two kids while her husband is thousands of miles away, fighting for our country on foreign soil.

Sam plops down next to me in the tiny chair and sets ten-month-old Brody on the carpeted floor beside her, giving him her car keys for entertainment before instructing Peyton to play with his brother for a little while so she can chat with me.

"I've had the longest day ever. First I got held up at work because the next nurse on shift was late, and then Brody threw up in the car after I picked him up from the sitter." Sam sighs. "It's days like these I really miss Josh. I just want to go home and take a nice long bath and go to bed. It would be nice if he was home and he could just take the kids for a while to give me time to decompress a bit."

"Sounds like you've had a rough one," I tell her. "You need me to come over and help out with the kids tonight so you can relax?"

Her green eyes brighten. "That would be amazing, but are you sure that won't interfere with your evening or anything? I don't want to be an imposition."

I roll my eyes. "Sam, please. You've met me, right? When am I ever busy?"

That causes her to frown, and I know exactly what she's thinking before she even says it. Sam doesn't like me being alone. "Have you talked to Wes?"

She asks me this nearly every day. By nature, she's a worrier, has been since I met her back in college when we got assigned to room together freshman year, and she hasn't changed since then.

I chew the inside of my lower lip and shake my head. "Not since he left last month. He's been sending me cards and different gifts, though, to let me know that he's still thinking about me."

She tilts her head, her pretty face etched with concern. "Have you decided if you're going to go through with the divorce?"

"Please, don't," I beg her quietly. "I know what you're going to say."

"Wes is a great guy. If you open up to him a little more and let him in, I think he could really be good for you. The two of you have so much history, and if anyone can help you move on, it's Wes."

She reaches over and places her hand on top of mine. "I only say it because I'm concerned about you. What you're putting yourself through—the inability to let go—it's not healthy. I want you to be happy, and maybe if you finally acknowledge that Jared isn't coming back, you'll be able to find love again. It's been five years, London, since anyone has heard from him, including his own mother. He's famous now—a different person from the one you knew. It's time to stop holding out for him. Face it, London. He's JJ White now. Jared Kraft is long gone."

Even though I've heard this speech from her so many times over the past five years, it doesn't make it any easier to swallow. The reality of the situation is that I'm in love with someone who doesn't love me back. It sucks and makes me seem a little crazy, but what can I do? I can't help the way I feel. There's never been anyone else for me, and I can't seem to "just get over it" like everyone keeps telling me to do.

My eyes burn as I try hard to fight back the tears. Within seconds, they're streaking down my face, and I quickly bat them away, ashamed that I'm still ridiculously emotional about the entire situation.

"Aw, London, I'm sorry. I don't mean to upset you. It kills me that you're still in all this pain."

I turn and give her a sad smile. "I'm okay, Sam. I promise. I just need more time, that's all. I think being with Wes was just too much of a reminder, you know? But I think that now that we're separated, I can start healing. I've never put much distance between me and the

Krafts because I love them so much, but I think in order to really heal, I'm going to have to cut my ties with all of them."

She gives my hand a little squeeze. "I'm here for you—whatever you need—always."

Her sweet words fill my heart with so much warmth, because I know without a doubt she means them. I never had any siblings growing up, but if I had to guess what it felt like to have a sister, this would be it.

## THEN
## LONDON

I grab a fresh-baked cookie off the plate and bite into pure chocolaty heaven. Jared's mom is an amazing baker. She even owns her own shop, making delicious treats. Over the last few years, I've done my best to learn everything I could from her about cooking since it's always been me and Dad at my place. I never really got the chance to learn much of that kind of stuff from my own mother, since she passed from breast cancer.

"You done real good with this batch, sweetie," Julie praises as she sits down next to me at the kitchen table. "Did you ever try making that meat loaf recipe I gave you?"

I swallow the delectable food in my mouth and then shake my head. "Not yet. Dad's been pulling double shifts on the weekends lately, and if he's not been doing that, he's been out on dates. I think getting back out there has taken his mind off the stress he always seems to be under at the station. He seems happier."

Julie raises her slender eyebrows. It's uncanny just how much Jared looks like his mother. They both have the same dark hair and bright blue eyes with smiles that could light up an entire room. Thin lines sprout out from the corners of her eyes, revealing that she has some age on her, but you would never know it, considering how active she is. The woman is always on the go and could probably run circles around me.

"Being a police officer has to be stressful, so I'm glad he's finding happiness. It's been a long time coming for him. He's been alone far too long." Julie takes a cookie off the plate for herself. "How do *you* feel about your father dating?"

I shrug. "It doesn't bother me. I mean, he's been single since Mom passed ten years ago. I think it's good that he's out there looking to find someone to spend his time with. The weekends are the only time that I'm around, and even then, Jared and I are always together."

She smiles. "You two have been attached at the hip for a while now, haven't you?"

"Nearly eight years," I confirm.

"Are the two of you thinking about the future?"

I furrow my brow. That's not the typical type of question she asks me. We rarely, if ever, discuss my and Jared's relationship, so it's odd that she would ask that out of the blue.

"No?" My own reply comes off sounding more like a question. "Why do you ask?"

"I don't mean to pry, dear. It's just that I couldn't help but notice that you're wearing a shiny new piece of jewelry on your left hand."

My heart instantly leaps into my throat.

Shit. Jared is going to be upset with me. He specifically asked me to not tell his mother anything because he wanted to be the one to break the news to her.

I quickly shove my hands onto my lap underneath the table. "Oh, um . . . that . . . we . . ."

She smiles. "It's okay, London. I already knew that he was going to ask you before you came in here wearing that ring."

I furrow my brow. "Did he tell you?"

She shakes her head. "Not exactly. When he came home last weekend, he left his dirty laundry sitting by his bed, and I found the receipt for the ring when I gathered up his clothes to wash them as a favor. He never intended on me finding the little slip of paper, so I laid it on the nightstand with his truck keys. I didn't want to let on that I knew until he was ready to tell me about his plans. It's no secret he's loved you since you two were kids. When did he ask you?"

A blush rushes to my cheeks, leaving them bright red, I'm sure. "Last night. It was a complete surprise. I meant to take the ring off before I came over. Jared wants to be the one to tell you and Henry. I think he's planning to tell the two of you today when his dad calls."

"It will make Henry and me both so happy to have you as a daughter-in-law. We always knew the two of you would get married someday. Henry told me a few weeks ago that he was glad that our son found you. You're a good girl, London, and we know that you'll do right by our son."

I bite my bottom lip as the tears begin to well up in my eyes. "Thank you. Being a part of your family means a lot to me. I think the world of you and Henry—Wes too—and I appreciate how much you've been there for me since Mom died. You've always been like a mother to me, so your approval means a lot."

She tilts her head and pats my cheek. "I already consider you a daughter."

The outpouring of love I feel from Julie overwhelms me. Unable to contain my emotions, I throw my arms around her and hug her tight. "You don't know how happy that makes me."

She rubs my back in such a caring way that it makes me miss my own mother, and suddenly I imagine what it would've been like had she still been here with me—how she would've reacted to the news of Jared and me getting married. Would she be just as ecstatic? I hope that she would've been. I'm sure she would have loved Jared just as much as I do.

"What's all this about?" Jared's voice catches me off guard, and I quickly pull away from his mom just in time to watch him stroll into the kitchen, wiping the grease off his hands with one of the shop towels from the garage.

Julie waves off her son dismissively and then winks at me. "Just a bit of girl talk." She gestures to the towel in his hands. "How're the repairs coming?"

Jared stuffs the towel in the back pocket of his stained jeans. "Slow, but I think I've nearly got it. It's running but still has a bit of a miss in it. I think I'll have it tuned up before Dad gets back. I can't wait to see the look on his face when he comes home and finds that I've finished the Nova for him."

She smiles. "I heard you fire it up out there. It sounded real good. Dad is going to be so pleased."

Jared's megawatt smile widens, and I swear my stomach flutters every time his dimples come out in full display. He's clearly excited to do this for his dad. It's something the two of them have been working on together since I've known Jared, so I know how much this means to him. This is the ultimate gift he could give his father— to show him how he thought of him while he was away by working every spare second he could on finishing this car.

I've never seen a father and son as close as Jared and Henry before. If they weren't working on Jared's pitching, which seemed to be their most favorite thing to do, they were working on the Nova or playing guitar together. I was always so amazed by that—the way they seemed to be best friends.

Jared makes his way over to the sink and scrubs the grime from his hands, using the orange hand cleaner, and says, "It's nearly four. Dad never calls so late. You don't think he's forgotten that it's Sunday, do you?"

Julie shakes her head. "I don't think that's possible. Your father loves hearing about your games far too much to forget about his Sunday call home."

He dries his hands on the faded kitchen towel hanging over the bottom cabinet door. "You're right. Maybe he had to work an odd shift or something. They've got MPs working some crazy hours over there."

"Military police are in high demand. They have to be around at all times," Julie reminds him.

Jared turns and kisses the top of my head as he takes a cookie off the plate before sitting next to me. "It sucks to not see him all the time. I miss him. I'll be so glad when he's back."

His mother reaches across the table and pats his arm. "Me too, son. Me too."

The afternoon drags on into the evening while we sit around the house and wait on Jared's father to call before we head back to the dorms. It's unusual for Henry to miss a phone call to his family, but it has happened before when he was out on some sort of mission with no access to a phone. He called late that night and spoke to Julie to let her know everything was okay and that he just got held up, so none of us is exactly alarmed that he hasn't called yet.

Wes enters the kitchen and leans back against the laminate countertop that covers the light maple cabinets. "I haven't missed his call, have I?"

Jared shakes his head. "No. Nothing yet."

Wes nods. "Where's Mom?"

"Upstairs getting ready for bed."

Wes sighs as he rakes his hand through the mess of blond hair on the top of his head. "It is getting late and I have an exam tomorrow.

I think I'm going to head back to campus and just call Mom tomorrow and get an update on Dad."

Jared nods as he glances up at the clock on the stove while his lips pull into a tight line. It's rare that Jared ever lets his emotions show, but the expression on his face clearly tells me that he's worried about his father. He's never been good at articulating if something is bothering him.

It's easy for me to relate to Jared missing his father.

Losing Mom when I was only ten rocked my entire world, and everything I ever knew was changed in an instant. While I was old enough at the time to understand what death was, I wasn't mature enough to realize how losing someone so important in your life would alter every part of your future.

My father became a different person after Mom died. He threw himself into his work to try and deflect the loneliness that he felt from losing his best friend. He once told me that staying idle for too long gives him far too much time to dwell on what he's lost. I think that's why he prefers to stay so busy, occupying his brain with a million tasks so he doesn't have to deal with the pain. Dad became a shell of the man I remember from before Mom died.

Dad took us to see a counselor for a short period when things became too much for him to deal with on his own. He thought it would be a good way for us to heal as a family. The one piece of advice that we got from those sessions that really seemed to resonate with Dad was that we have to find ways to move on—that the only way to truly heal is to keep on living even though our grief sometimes seems like it's more than we can bear and that our loved ones wouldn't want us to go into a dark place emotionally because they've passed on.

"If you want to stay, Jared, I'll drive London back to campus with me." Wes's voice drags me out of my thoughts.

Jared pushes back from the table, causing the wood chair to

squeak against the linoleum flooring before he stands. "No. I'll take her, but call me if you hear anything."

Wes nods. "Will do, brother."

Jared reaches down and extends his hand to me. "Ready?"

I take his hand and stand beside him.

Wes's eyes flick down to Jared's and my joined hands, and his lips twist as he fixes his gaze on my left hand. His eyebrows pull inward, and the expression on his face makes it seem like he's upset before his eyes jerk up to meet mine. He gives me a small smile. "Nice ring."

I raise my brow. I had completely forgotten about my ring, but when I look to Jared, he's staring at his brother through narrowed eyes.

Feeling a little uneasy, I find myself unsure of how to respond. "Um, thanks."

Jared doesn't say a word and doesn't elaborate any more on the topic.

Wes's shoulders sag a bit when it becomes clear that he's not getting any further explanation. "See you around, London."

"Bye," I reply as Jared pulls me through the kitchen toward the front door, not giving me time to say much else.

"Mom, we're leaving!" Jared calls up the stairs.

Julie walks to the top of the landing of the split-level stairs and frowns. "I'm sorry your dad didn't get to hear about the game. I'll tell him all about it for you when he calls."

"Let me know what he says after he finds out we ran all over Ole Miss last night. He'll get a kick out of that."

She smiles. "I will. You two have a safe ride back to school, and I'll call you tomorrow while I'm at work at the shop, Jared, and let you know what Dad said."

## NOW
## LONDON

Sitting down for dinner in this house hasn't felt the same in the last few years. It's not that I don't like Dad's new wife, or that I'm not appreciative of how happy she makes him, but it doesn't feel like home to me anymore. Sylvia is nice and has always treated me very well, but it's a definite fact that she's the most important woman in Dad's life now.

From the moment she moved in, she started changing things around in the house to suit her tastes. For instance, Mom always kept the silverware in the drawer next to the sink because she liked to hand wash the dishes since she didn't trust that the dishwasher got them clean enough, whereas Sylvia feels the silverware should go on the other side of the dishwasher because that's why she has the appliance—to make life easy. It's almost as if Dad went out and found the polar opposite of Mom.

I so want to tell Sylvia that life isn't easy—that it's hard—and she doesn't have to pretend it is around me. I've been through so much, so I can personally attest to the fact that, even when things seem easy, at any moment they can blow up in your face and prove once again just how shitty life can be and how we're meant to struggle on this earth. It's better to not try and pretend things are any other way.

"London, honey, will you pass the peas?" Sylvia asks from across the table with a smile on her face.

I do as she asks and still find myself deep in thought about Mom. I wish she was here. It would be nice to be able to talk to her about things going on in my life.

"You okay, sweetie?" Dad's voice pulls me out of my thoughts as I continue to push the pile of peas around on my plate with my fork, just as I did when I was a kid.

I glance up and make eye contact with him. "I'm fine. Just thinking."

Dad nods, while his hazel eyes linger on me. "About Wes?"

"No. Not about him." My voice comes out in a hushed tone.

It's hard for me to talk about Wes. Every time I think about him, it reminds me of how awful I've been to him lately. I've done my best to ignore him, but he keeps sending candy from his mother's shop. It's like he wants to keep himself at the forefront of my mind. Wes wants things to work out between us so badly, but deep down I know I won't ever get past the fact that he's the brother of the man I once loved with every piece of my heart.

I should never have gotten involved with Wes, but it was so easy to allow myself to believe the charade that I could get over Jared by being with Wes. Being with Wes was comfortable—easy—because I had known him just as long as I had known Jared.

"I spoke to Julie the other day. I know you and Wes were only married a few months, but he's taking the split hard," Dad tells me.

I sit there silently. I'm not sure what he expects me to say. I understand that I'm the cause of Wes's pain, but I also know there's no simple way to fix what I've put him through. It's not like he was blind to the situation when he got involved with me. He knew I was broken. He knew I was already having a hard time getting over Jared and moving on. He knew there was a great possibility that us being together would never work, yet he was willing to try anyway.

That was a mistake.

We both knew how hard it would be to be together, but at the time the chance of finding happiness—and, God, did I want that—outweighed the probable dark future that lay ahead of us once we started down that path.

"When have you spoken to him last?" I close my eyes and take a deep breath and will myself not to cry as Dad keeps questioning me about Wes.

I feel bad enough already. Dad trying to pry and point out the obvious isn't helping. Wes wants more than I'm able to give him.

"London?" I open my eyes at the sound of Dad's voice.

"I haven't spoken to him in over a month. I think it's best if we keep our distance for a while."

Dad's gaze flicks over to Sylvia, and her typical bright smile turns into a frown. It only takes a moment, but I can tell the expression they share between them means they're worried about something.

Then, as if right on cue, a knock sounds at the door. I glance over at Dad, who doesn't look a bit concerned and pops another bite of steak into his mouth. When I look to Sylvia, she simply shrugs, causing me to sigh as I pull the napkin off my lap and toss it down on the table.

"I'll get it," I say as I push back from the table.

As I walk toward the front door, a feeling in the pit of my stomach eats away at me. I don't like surprises, and I have the feeling that's exactly what I'm about to step into.

When I open the door, my heart leaps into my throat, and every word in my vocabulary leaves me as my eyes land on Wes, standing on the porch with a dozen yellow roses in one hand and a box of his mother's chocolate-covered strawberries in the other. Wes is dressed in a pair of gray slacks, a white button-down dress shirt, and a tie, so I can tell he's rushed over from his office to make it here.

A sheepish smile ghosts across his face. "I hope it's okay that I'm here. Your dad invited me for dinner."

I should've expected something like this from Dad. Whenever there is an issue going on in my life, he always tries to fix it. I guess my broken marriage is his newest challenge.

I lick my lips and step back, allowing him room to come inside, hating that my father is trying to play Mr. Fix-It with my love life, but I can't fault him for wanting to help. "It's fine. Come on in."

His tall frame eases into the doorway, and he hands me the roses. "I know these candies are your favorite. Mom whipped them up for me before I came over."

I take the flowers and the small box with a small smile of gratitude. "They're lovely. Your mom makes the best desserts in town."

Wes smiles. "She didn't name it Best Candies for nothing."

I allow a little laugh to slip through, and he winks.

It's nice that he's trying to lighten up the tenseness of this situation, but it's difficult to deny the tension that's still between us. The best thing I can do is be gracious and make it through this dinner without things getting weird.

"Come on in, Wes!" Dad calls from the other room, not really giving me the option to disinvite him. "We've got a place set up for you."

Wes and I walk around the corner to find Sylvia setting another place across from Dad at the small wooden table.

She glances up at me and bites her bottom lip with an expression that I can only describe as her saying sorry. I wave her off from behind Wes so that he can't see me and then take my seat again. This setup has Dad written all over it.

"This looks amazing, Mrs. Uphill," Wes compliments Sylvia.

She smiles and passes him the bowl of mashed potatoes. "Thank you, and remember, it's just Sylvia, please. I insist."

He nods and takes the bowl before piling a healthy portion onto his plate, making himself quite comfortable.

We all begin eating silently. I mean, I'm not sure what I'm even supposed to say in this situation. The whole idea of splitting up our marriage was to get some space between us. Wes should have known I wouldn't be cool with him just popping over like this. You would think he would know me better, and would know that he should have at least warned me first. A simple phone call would've sufficed.

Dad clears his throat. "How's work going, Wes? Last I heard you were getting some big promotion."

Wes wipes his mouth with his napkin. "Oh, yes, sir. The firm assigned me to be the head engineer on a project for the downtown Knoxville area."

"That's wonderful," Sylvia says, her voice full of admiration. "To be so young and to already have so much responsibility—they must know how intelligent you are."

"Thank you," Wes replies, and there's a hint of red in his cheeks.

He always gets a little embarrassed when he's thrust into the limelight, which is the exact opposite of his brother, who reveled in it.

*Gah!* I mentally scold myself for yet again comparing Wes to Jared. It's a bad habit I've yet to figure out how to break.

Dad grins. "That's great news, Wes. Means you've got a real bright future in front of you, which is good news, considering when you and London start a family you'll be financially stable."

"Dad!" I instantly retort, trying my best to head him off before he continues down the path of fixing Wes and me into his ideal of a perfect little family.

"What?" Dad asks defensively. "Aren't I allowed to discuss all the good things that your future might hold?"

"No," I say instantly.

He lifts one eyebrow. "Why not?"

"Wes and I aren't together anymore. That's why. You know that. I don't know why you're going on like we are."

The second the words leave my mouth, my eyes dash over to Wes. Pain flickers across his face, and once again I'm reminded of how shitty a human being I am for continuing to hurt him. I can't take this—sitting in this room one second longer—dragging out a relationship that I know is over. I can't sit here and worry that I'm going to say the wrong thing at any moment and hurt Wes all over again. He doesn't deserve that.

I shove away from the table and throw my napkin down. "I'm sorry. I can't do this."

I turn toward the front door and race through it. I know I'm being a coward—that I should be braver and face up to Wes about how I've treated him—but I just can't. I know that's wrong of me, but I don't know what else to do.

The night air hits me as soon as I'm outside, and a chill rushes up my spineless back.

"London, wait up!" Wes calls from behind me, but I keep trudging forward until I make it to my car, which is parked along the curb out in front of my father's house.

I hit the key fob and the lights flash, letting me know I've unlocked it.

"London, please," Wes begs, but I don't stop.

I shake my head. "I'm sorry, Wes. I can't have this conversation with you right now."

He steps beside me and places his hand on the car door, not allowing me to open it. "Won't you just talk to me? What happened back there?"

Tears instantly streak down my face, and there's no way I can hold them back. "I'm no good for you, Wes. You deserve better than me. Don't you see that? Why do you keep trying to hold on to this relationship? It's never going to work."

He shakes his head. "No. London, I deserve you. I always have. If Jared hadn't been in the way—"

"Stop!" I command. "Don't bring *him* up."

"I have to," he says. "He's the reason we're having problems. Hell, he's not even around anymore and I still can't escape living in my little brother's shadow."

"You're not living in his shadow."

He shakes his head. "But I am. I always wanted you. I've always been the right brother for you, but you, just like everyone else, got wrapped up in Jared's charms and couldn't see how much I've always loved you. You never paid any attention to me until he was gone. I was background noise until he decided to walk out on all of you."

"We've always been friends, Wes. Always. But you knew that I loved your brother. You know how much he meant to me."

Wes throws his hands into the air. "God, I can't believe you still love him after all this time. When are you going to face it, London? He's gone. He left you—me—hell, even his own mother. He never gave two shits about any of us. I figured that out the minute he left us behind to start a new life. We were all hurting, and he didn't care about anyone but himself." Wes's eyes stare into mine. "It's time you realize you're waiting on a ghost—a memory of the person you thought he was. He's moved on, and I wish you could too, and when you do, I want it to be with me. Please, London, I love you. I always have. Think about what we could have if you let him go."

My mouth grows dry as I absorb every word he says. He's right—I know he is—and everything he said is the truth, but how can I make him understand that Jared was my soul mate, and there's no easy way to fill the hole made when your other half is ripped away without any explanation?

"Wes . . ." I chew on the inside of my lower lip as I search for the right words to say. "I just need more time, and I know that's unfair to ask of you, but that's what I need. I can't be with you and not think of him."

He sighs deeply while a frown pulls at the corners of his mouth. "If time and space are what you need, then I'll give that to you. I know you've been through a lot. I've been with you through it all, so I understand. When you're ready to talk about things and where we stand, call me, and we'll figure all this out."

His words are saying that he's all right with the situation, but I know this is killing him. It's written all over his face.

"Thank you," is all I can manage to say.

Wes has always been the thoughtful and understanding Kraft boy. He was the one who worked in his mother's shop for hours on end because she needed the extra help. He was the one who volunteered at the animal shelter to nurture the sick and abandoned pets that people no longer wanted. He's also the brother who held what was left of his family together when tragedy struck. Like my dad, Wes is a fixer, and I guess when he saw how broken I was five years ago, he made it his mission to put me back together.

We stand there in silence. No words need to be said for us each to know the other is hurting. I wish I could end his pain, but there's no easy way to stop loving somebody.

"I've got to go," I tell him as I place my hand on the handle of the car door.

He nods and takes a step back, allowing me space to open the door. "Call me if you need anything."

"Okay." It's the last thing I tell him before I jump in my car and speed away, wondering if there's even a way to fix something as broken as my smashed-up heart.

### THEN
### JARED

**M**y fingers glide over the strings as I play the chorus of "Simple Man" on my Gibson. I love this old guitar. It was a high school graduation present from Dad, and I remember the note he wrote and wove through the strings when he gave it to me: *Now you have your own. Don't bother asking if you can take mine to college in the fall.*

I still laugh every time I think about that. There's no way of counting how many hours I logged on his guitar, but I know it's enough that I can play just about any song after hearing it one time. For my sixteenth birthday, Dad bought me some lessons, and he was proud when the instructor told him that I had a natural ear for music. Of course, though, Dad made it well known that playing the guitar was merely a hobby for me and not a career path that I could even consider.

Baseball was my destiny. Even as a junior in high school I captured the eye of college scouts. Dad was right. Baseball is my future. I'm good at it, and it looks as though I have an amazing career in front of me.

London lies on her side, watching me intently as I continue to play and begin to sing to her while we sit on a blanket in the grass just in front of my dorm. The rasp in my voice is on point, and soon a small crowd begins gathering around us.

It's like this every time I sing, students stopping on their way to class to listen to me cover songs that I love.

I close my eyes and project my voice, making sure even the people behind the crowd can hear me.

I like being the center of attention. It makes me feel good, knowing that I'm entertaining people, whether that's on the field or just me sitting here playing this guitar and singing.

When I finish playing the last chord, the horde of people around us begins clapping and cheering, shouting out for me to play another. I smile at all of them and do as requested. Like the last one, it's another slow rock ballad. Those songs seem to fit my voice best, and I learned a lot of the classics from Dad.

When I finish the second one, once again the crowd cries for me to keep playing, but I simply shake my head and laugh.

I set my guitar back in the case and then wrap my arms around London. "Have to get some study time in with my girl here. I've distracted her long enough."

A few of the girls sigh heavily before walking off. Some even tell London that she's a lucky girl, which makes her smile proudly.

London sits up and then busies herself with pulling out a few textbooks from her bag and spreading them out on the blanket.

I reach out and grab one of the books and then glance up just in time to find a petite girl staring at me intently from about twenty feet away. Her short, jet-black hair has a bright pink stripe in the bangs while the rest of her clothes scream grunge, and I find it odd that she's just staring at me so blatantly. Goth chicks aren't usually so enamored of jocks like me.

I break eye contact with the girl, giving her a chance to look away too, but when I check again, she's still staring at me. She takes a couple steps toward us and then plops down on the grass in front of London and me without any sort of invitation.

I raise my eyebrows as the girl tilts her head as if to get a better look at me.

"I can't figure you out," the girl says as she narrows one of her heavily made-up eyelids. "Are you a jock or are you a musician?"

My brow furrows instantly at her question. "What do you mean?"

"I mean," she says with a sigh, "musicians live and breathe their music, and it bleeds into every facet of their life. Most guys that look like Abercrombie models aren't deep enough to be believable when they sing, but you, you're different. I can feel your emotion when you sing, and that's not something that can be faked."

I laugh. "That's a little stereotypical, don't you think?"

She shrugs. "Maybe, but a true musician puts his craft in front of everything else. I just don't think it's fair to the rest of us who don't look like you. You shouldn't be allowed to be gifted in more than one thing."

"Um . . ." I sit there stunned and glance over at London, who simply shrugs. This girl floors me. She's so forward that she almost comes off as rude. I don't think she means to be, but I don't know how to react to her. "Thanks, I think?"

She shoves herself up to her feet. "Oh, that was definitely a compliment. Here." She reaches into the back pocket of her jean shorts and pulls out a business card and then hands it to me. "I'm in a band called Lick Me and Split. If you ever want to gig with us, we can always use another guitar player. You should know I don't make this offer to just anyone. Only people I think are truly amazing."

I take the card, glancing down at the picture of a seductive tongue poking through a pair of ruby-red lips, and chuckle. "Nice."

"Isn't it? Guys seem to like it. Call us if you ever want to jam. Later."

And just as fast as she appeared, the petite rocker chick is gone, blending in with the crowds milling about on the lawn on this beautiful fall day.

"That was odd." London's voice pulls my attention back to her.

I laugh and couldn't agree with her more, but I seize the opportunity to poke a little fun at the situation. "Yeah, but it's nice to know that someone thinks I have some talent."

London giggles, and her green eyes light up as she leans in to kiss my lips. "I can tell you for a fact that you're talented in more areas than just baseball."

I cradle her head in my hands and study the delicate contours of her features. Her slender nose fits perfectly on her heart-shaped face, and her cheeks are flushed from the kiss we just shared.

I trace my thumb over her plump bottom lip. "Thank you for believing in me. It means the world to me that you do."

She smiles. "I'll always be by your side, no matter what—baseball, using your business degree at a nine-to-five job, or even trying to make a living playing that guitar that you love so much. I'm not going anywhere."

I nip at her bottom lip. "I love you."

"I love you too."

Our relationship is easy and natural, like breathing. I can see a clear-cut future with her. A life that stays simple, just like it is now—no matter how my life turns out.

London and I study outside the rest of the afternoon without interruption. It's not until I check the time that I notice it's nearly four, and I begin to wonder what Dad had to say about the game yesterday. "I think I should call Mom."

London looks up from her book. "Okay. Let me just pack my books up and we can take off."

We walk hand in hand back to the dorm, chatting about classes and my upcoming game against the University of Kentucky.

When we step up onto the stoop of her building, I lean in and give her a quick peck before telling her I will call her after I speak with Mom so we can decide on a place to eat for dinner tonight.

Once I'm in my own room, I pick up the phone and dial Mom. The phone rings over and over without an answer, and then it hits me. She's probably still at the shop, working on orders. That happens from time to time since she's a one-woman show in the place. She takes all the orders, does all the baking, makes the candies, practically everything except for deliveries. An older gentleman named Bud does that just to have something to do because he's retired. He insists he loves the job because he likes brightening other people's days.

I dial the candy shop, and that phone too goes unanswered, which is odd because Mom is a creature of habit. She rarely strays from either of those two locations unless she needs to get groceries for the house or run an errand or two.

I open my book and attempt to pass the time, but I can't focus. Another hour passes, and then I try Mom again, and I'm too anxious to wait much longer. I try both the home and the shop numbers, and again they both go unanswered.

An odd feeling comes over me, and my thoughts turn to a dark place. What if something happened to her? With both me and Wes away at school, she's all alone since Dad's out on deployment. She could have fallen down the stairs carrying a basket of laundry and gotten hurt, and there's no one there to help her.

My heart races beneath my ribs, and the urge to drive out there and check on her overwhelms me, but before I get too crazy with worry, I need to make one more phone call.

Wes answers on the third ring. "Hello?"

"Hey, man. Have you heard from Mom today?" I ask.

"No, but I was just thinking about calling her to find out what happened to Dad's call yesterday. Did you talk to her?"

"I haven't, and I tried to call her a couple times today but got no answer. I'm starting to worry about her. I'm thinking I may drive out to the house and check on her."

"I'll come with you. Pick me up in five?" he asks.

"Yeah, let me just grab London and we'll be on our way."

Once I call London and explain what's going on, she agrees that we need to go check on Mom just to be safe. I can tell by the tone in her voice that she's worried too, because it's unlike Mom to be unreachable for so long.

London is already waiting for me on the stoop of her dorm when I get there. When I pull up in front of her, she hops into the passenger side and immediately slides over next to me on the bench seat. "Wes ready?"

I nod as I glance over at her beautiful face. Her eyes hold a million questions in them—questions I'm just as anxious as she is to discover the answers to. "We'll pick him up and then be on our way."

London places her hand on top of mine and gives it a gentle squeeze. "I'm sure everything will be okay. Maybe she's just sick and sleeping and didn't hear the phone ring."

I sigh. "I hope you're right."

It doesn't take long before we arrive at Wes's apartment. My brother is sitting on the steps leading to his front door, and when he sees my truck, he pushes himself up and then dusts his hands off on the front of his jeans before he hops inside.

Wes's attention immediately falls on London, and his gaze trails up and down her body as he checks her out in the jean shorts and red T-shirt she's wearing. "Hey, London. How ya doin'?"

If I wasn't already going out of my mind with worry, I might be tempted to call my brother out for looking at my girl the way he has been lately. He needs to stop that shit.

London gives him a tight-lipped smile as I hit the gas and set out for home. "Nervous. It's unlike Julie to go MIA. I called Dad to go check on her, but he's working, pulling a double shift patrolling some wrestling event that's in town, and won't be finished until late."

"Brian has been working a lot lately, hasn't he?" Wes asks, attempting to make small talk. It seems that he's also trying to distract himself from thinking about what could be stopping Mom from answering her phone all day.

London sighs. "Yeah, but he says the extra money helps. I think he likes it for when he goes out on all these dates. He keeps telling me that he forgot how expensive women are."

Wes laughs. "That's why you don't see me dating much. Being a poor college guy sucks."

"You don't date much because no one can put up with your crabby ass." I laugh as I tease my brother over his lack of game. He's never been a smooth talker with the ladies. It's like he gets nervous and clams up around them, but when he does work up the courage to ask someone out, he always finds reasons to get rid of them pretty quickly. "You can't keep a girl around longer than a week."

He shrugs. "I haven't found the right girl yet. Not everyone out there is as perfect as the one you've got."

I grin and throw my arm around London's shoulders, driving home the fact that she is indeed mine before I pull her in tighter against me while keeping the other hand on the steering wheel. "Well, you can't have this one. This perfect woman is all mine."

"Stop." London pokes me in the ribs, and I laugh at how flushed her face is.

I stare down into her green eyes. "What? It's true. I don't share well, especially when it comes to you."

I notice out of the corner of my eye that Wes is no longer looking at us but staring out the passenger-side window. It's not like I purposefully try to hurt his feelings, but I want to make it clear that whatever little crush he's harboring for my girl, he's going to have to squash it quickly before it starts pissing me the fuck off. I know London is beautiful and damn near perfect, and I'm sure it's hard to not be attracted to that, because, hell, I know I'm pretty damn addicted to her myself, but he can never have her. No matter how much he may want to.

We're all quiet for the rest of the trip, all of us contemplating the things on our minds, like what held up Dad's call yesterday and why Mom isn't picking up her phone.

I press my foot down a little more on the gas, breaking all the speed limits as my mind begins to wander to that dark place again. I just pray to God that nothing has happened to her, because I'm not sure what I'd do if anything ever happened to my parents— either of them.

## NOW
## JARED

**A** sea of sweat-riddled bodies jumps in time with the beat. It's truly a sight I never dreamed I would see, and it amazes me that these people are all here for my band.

Playing in front of a sold-out crowd is one of the best feelings in the world. It's the only place I can be lately where my mind totally shuts off while the music and the energy of the crowd overtake my body. The coolest thing in the world is when everyone seems to know your name simply because you can play the shit out of an instrument.

I shred the last few riffs on the guitar as Ace belts out the lyrics to the crowd, and thousands of people join in with him, knowing every single word. Ace streaks past me like lightning in the all-white clothing that Jane Ann insists we wear as part of the marketing push behind the band's name, Wicked White. After nearly four years, I'm getting pretty damn tired of this all-white clothes bullshit.

I would love to say that I'm not jealous of Ace, but the truth is that I'm consumed with jealousy. Admitting that I want what Ace has makes me feel like a complete asshole, but there's no way I can deny it, even to myself, and I'm sure everyone around me sees it too.

One day Ace is going to screw up, and when he does, I'll be there to take his spot as front man of this band and prove that I was the best choice all along.

As the last beat of a song plays, Ace throws his hand in the air, waving, and the crowd goes wild, begging for more. "We're Wicked White! Thank you!"

I shove my hair out of my eyes as I remove the strap from around my neck and hand Joe, one of our roadies, the white guitar I played during the show.

"Nice playing, Jared," Joe says as he tucks a strand of his sandy-blond hair behind his ear. "You guys were really in sync tonight. The best live playing I've heard from you all."

"Thanks, man. It's taken us a while. It's hard at times to get us all on the same page off the stage, but for some reason when we get in front of a live audience, we just come together. Wanting to get the music perfect is about the only thing we all agree on."

Joe nods and then pats me on the back. "Whatever it is, it's working for you. You guys keep sounding like that, and we'll have a set job for a long, long time."

When I step backstage, Ace is nowhere to be found, but my other two bandmates, Tyler and Luke, are waiting for me. These two aren't what I would exactly consider my friends, but they definitely like me more than they like Ace.

Luke grins and his face lights up the moment we make eye contact. "Dude, we're all going out tonight. There's some strip club here in town that's supposed to have chicks with fantastic tits and incredible food. You in?"

I hesitate before I answer. Typically when the band is on the road, I can be found in the hotel bar drinking myself into oblivion.

I rarely go out. Having lighthearted fun isn't something I'm into anymore. I'm too fucked up to be able to enjoy myself, because I have to constantly live with the guilt of my past and how I treated the people in my life who once loved me. I don't do relationships of any kind anymore. They're too painful, and I know that nothing ever goes right, so there's no use in trying to pretend that there's a happily ever after waiting for me.

Luke shoves his hands deep into the front pockets of his jeans while he awaits my answer.

I shake my head. "Naw, man. I'm beat. I think I'm going back to my room to crash. You guys have fun."

He sighs. "All right, then. We'll catch you later."

When they walk away, I grab the hem of my shirt and pull it up to wipe the sweat from my face. Running around on stage fires me up, reminding me that I'm still alive, and is really one of the only things that gets my blood pumping these days. The second I drop it back down, I find Jane Ann walking directly toward me with a smile on her face.

"Well, I see our last little chat about getting your shit together is working. I was glad to find you here on time and sober—ready to perform and back Ace up like you should. If you keep working together like this, I see huge things in the band's future. Wicked White could turn into one of the biggest bands to hit the scene in a long, long time if you all can learn to play nice with one another."

I fight hard to keep from rolling my eyes at her. "What makes you think we can be that huge? The music we're playing sounds exactly like every other thing on the radio."

"Exactly!" she says, the excitement in her voice clear as day. "On the radio, we blend in but stand out enough to be noticed. Wicked White's music is getting so much play in the top forty right now. What really sets you all apart are your looks. Dressing all in white is a perfect gimmick to make people remember you, and once they start remembering you, they'll start following you. Hell, you're all good-looking guys too, and that certainly doesn't hurt. I wouldn't be surprised if Ace gets voted sexiest man alive at some point in time, and when that happens sales will explode."

"Who gives a shit about getting on the cover of some magazine?" I grumble.

"I do!" she says. "Don't you know how much publicity that will throw onto the band? Not only will the people who listen to the pop stations know you, but the rest of the world as well."

"Why would it be Ace? It could easily be me if you would allow me to sing on a few tracks," I quickly retort.

"Look, Jared. We've been over this. You being front man for this band is never going to happen. You're not the leader type. Ace has a calm demeanor and everyone loves him. When the two of you get into it, he's the one with the more level head. That's the kind of man we need fronting this band."

I roll my eyes. "I get so sick of hearing you praise Ace while putting the rest of us down at the same time. How do you know that he's the right man for the job? The guy rarely speaks to any of us, and when he does it's to belittle someone else, namely me, and make it seem like his ability to create music is far superior to mine, and I don't appreciate that one damn bit."

Jane Ann sighs. "Look, Jared. I'm not going to stand here and have this same argument with you again. We've gone over this a million times. The label and I have chosen Ace. The decision has been made, and if you haven't noticed, the crowd loves him. Hell, the ticket sales are proving that we've made the right choice. You just have to get over the fact that you'll never be the one in charge—the one in the spotlight. You might've been the 'it' guy when it came to playing on the field, but in this business—in this band—Ace is the man. Get used to it."

My nostrils flare and my cheeks grow hot, no doubt turning my face red. It pisses me off when she acts like I'm supposed to be okay with sitting back and playing second fiddle when this wasn't what I was promised, but it looks like there's nothing I can do about the choice they've made if I want to stay in this band. "Fine, but don't be surprised when shit doesn't work out with Ace. I don't think the guy has what it takes to be a real leader, and he will eventually fuck this band over."

I don't give her a chance to say anything else to me. I can't stand here and listen to her talk about how I'm not good enough one more minute.

I quickly find a ride back to the hotel, needing my space from the whole Wicked White scene. I spend most of my time alone. I don't do well with people—not anymore. My only friend in this world is Jack, and I'm glad that I can pretty much find him at any bar in the world.

I plop down at the hotel bar, and the middle-aged guy with a graying goatee behind it greets me. "What are you drinking?"

I lay three one-hundred-dollar bills on the marble bar top. "Jack. Make it a double and keep them coming until I'm barely able to ride the elevator back up to my room."

The man's brown eyes flick down to the money, and he nods. He doesn't ask any questions as he pulls out two glasses, and I'm thankful for that. I'm sure he sees his fair share of people who come to drink to forget the shit in their lives. "You got it."

It's times like these when I feel the most alone. Whenever I had a problem before, I would just tell London about it, and together we'd figure out a solution. If she were in my life right now, I would be filling her ear with the bullshit that Jane Ann and Ace have been pulling on me lately.

I sigh as I pick up the drink in front of me. That girl . . . she's irreplaceable. Not only was London the love of my life but my best friend too. I don't think I'll ever get over her. The best I can ever hope for is finding a distraction to keep my mind off of her.

The cool glass rolls against my lips as I tip my head back and shoot the fiery liquid down my throat and then immediately follow it with the other glass. The burn is comforting. It wasn't the right choice, learning to deal with my problems by drowning them with alcohol, I know that, but it was the only thing that worked to take the pain away for just a little while. I have a hard time forgetting how fucked up everything got since the day my entire world was rocked. Since that day I've learned that I can't be a burden on anyone else but me—that I can't put my problems on someone else, because that will only make them miserable too.

The bartender quickly refills my glasses, and those disappear just as fast. It's not until I've drunk away my first hundred dollars that I notice an attractive woman in her late thirties watching me from two stools down. She's turned her chair toward me, crossed her toned, slender legs in my direction, and is making no attempt to hide the fact that she's studying me intently. Her long brown hair falls over her shoulders in soft waves. When I lock my gaze with hers, she grabs the pick holding the olive in her martini and wraps her lips seductively around the little green ball before sucking it off the stick.

There's no mistaking what this woman wants from me. I've been through this more times than I care to admit over the past few years.

With that said, I'm still a man, and I have needs. I've learned to never turn away a hot piece of ass that's willing and very eager to please me. Every conquest I've had as of late has been a random lonely woman at the hotel bar. It's convenient for me to offer to go to their room and fuck their brains out. Most of them are alone on business trips, and I'm sure they've got husbands or boyfriends back home waiting for them, but I don't care. I'll never see them again, so no one will ever know about their one-night tryst with a rock star.

It will just be a memory for them. One they use to get themselves off every now and then when they think about me while their poor schmuck of a husband fucks them.

My affairs never get publicized, and I'm thankful for the privacy. That's one of the reasons fucking soccer moms is a smart move—they're hell-bent on keeping their night with me a secret too.

I meet her stare and lick my lips slowly, in a way to make sure she gets that I'm reading her signals loud and clear. "Can I buy you a drink?"

She smiles and stands up. My eyes trace the contours of her body as she swishes her hips in her tight black skirt. This woman is practically in heat, her body begging for me to make it feel good.

She takes the seat next to me and then bites her lower lip. "Sure, lover."

I glance in the bartender's direction and point down to the lady's nearly empty glass, and then hold up my index finger.

The woman beside me doesn't waste any time as she places her hand on my inner thigh and leans in to whisper in my ear, giving me a straight shot down her form-fitting blouse so I can see that she doesn't have a bra on. "You're so sexy in person, and I'm a huge fan who would love to show you a little appreciation. Have you ever been with an older woman?"

For some reason thinking they are the first older woman I've ever been with excites them. They get off on the whole Mrs. Robinson thing. I'm sure in this woman's mind she's about to show me just how good being with an older woman can be, so I'll pretend with her, just like I do each and every time, that she's my very first older lover.

I graze my teeth over my bottom lip and allow my eyes to dip down to her tits before I pull my gaze back up to meet hers. "No, but you sure look like a mom I'd like to fuck."

Her ruby-red lips pull apart as she grins, loving my answer. "What would you say if I asked you to come up to my room for a bit of fun, then?"

I raise my eyebrows. This one definitely isn't a bit bashful, and my brain turns with the possibilities of all the freaky shit this woman might be into. Fucking her will be a damn good time. I can already tell.

Sex has become another distraction for me. In the moment all I can think about is finding my own release, and the memories of my past stay far away for that brief time. More than anything, all I want to do is forget—forget how I walked out on everyone who ever gave a damn about me like they didn't matter to me anymore.

I twist my lips like I'm contemplating her offer, but then I give her the grin she's been waiting for, letting her know she's about to get exactly what she's practically begging me for.

Her face lights up with a seductive smile before her hand drifts over to my crotch and she traces her fingers along the long, hard bulge beneath my jeans. "I'll take that as a yes."

I tip one last shot back and then grab her hand, pulling her off the stool toward the elevators, not giving her time to tease me any more. It's time for her to make good on all the promises of pleasure she's been dangling in front of me.

I press the up button and glance down at the woman. "Room number?"

"Five thirty-five," she answers as we step inside the empty elevator and she hits the button for the fifth floor.

When the doors shut us inside alone, I yank her to me and crush my lips against hers, not giving her any time to speak. I'm not feeling up to any conversation tonight. This woman will be a perfect distraction, and I'm so ready to lose myself for a little while.

## THEN
## LONDON

**W**hen we pull into our neighborhood, dread flows through my veins. I've had a bad feeling ever since Jared told me this evening that he wasn't able to get in contact with Julie. As long as I've known her, she's always been available to her boys.

Jared grips the steering wheel so tight that his knuckles turn white, and even though he's not saying it, I can tell he's nervous.

I pat his hand. "I'm sure she's all right."

I'm not sure who I'm trying to convince more, Jared or myself, at this point.

As we drive past my house, I notice it's completely dark inside, which doesn't surprise me because Dad is still working his double. All the other houses we pass have lights on, illuminating the inside for the families who are home. Jared's house comes into view, and oddly, all the lights are on in there as well.

Wes leans forward as if to get a closer look and runs his hand through his blond hair. "Looks like she's there."

Jared pulls the truck into the drive and throws the transmission up into park. "Wonder where she's been all day. She knew we were planning on calling, so she had to realize we'd worry once we couldn't reach her."

Wes nods as he opens the car door. "Agreed, she's probably fine. Maybe we overreacted for nothing."

Jared sighs. "I hope you're right." He turns to me. "Ready?"

We all file out of the truck, and Jared threads his fingers through mine after he shuts the door. We walk up the sidewalk, and when we reach the door, Wes turns the knob to find it unlocked, as if Julie was expecting us.

Wes glances back at Jared, his brown eyes worried. Jared frowns, and the concerned expression he wore on the way over here returns. Julie is a fanatic about locking her door, especially since she's been alone so much lately with Henry being overseas and both of her sons away at college.

Wes pushes the door open and instantly calls out, "Mom? You here?"

We all wait with bated breath as we step over the threshold. No answer comes, and Jared tightens his grip on my hand.

Wes tries again. "Mom?"

When he doesn't get an answer, he rushes toward the kitchen with Jared and me right on his heels.

As we turn the corner we see Julie sitting at the head of the table with a vacant expression on her face. She's not moving—it's like she's so lost in thought she doesn't even realize we've been calling her name.

Jared releases my hand and rushes over to his mom's side and drops to his knees beside her. "Mom?" His voice is barely above a whisper, as if to not frighten her. With a slightly shaky hand, he reaches up to her forearm that's resting on the table in front of her. "Can you hear me? What's wrong?"

Jared's touch causes her to flinch like he startled her from a deep trance. Julie turns her face toward Jared, and the first thing that draws my attention is just how red and swollen her eyes are. It looks like she's been crying for days. "Jared? When did you get here?"

Despite his calm exterior, Jared's blue eyes are full of panic as he flicks them up toward his brother's face. It's easy for me to read him because I've known him for so long and know pretty much what he's thinking. Even though he looks calm, he's panicking inside.

Wes steps up next to me and wraps his arm around my shoulders like he's bracing himself as Jared turns his attention back to Julie.

"We were calling your name. Didn't you hear us?" Jared asks.

She slowly shakes her head. "I guess I didn't."

He draws in a slow breath and then releases it, doing his best to stay calm as he tries to get to the bottom of the situation. "Are you hurt?"

She frowns. "No."

The muscles tense in Jared's back beneath his dark T-shirt. "Is Dad okay?"

Wes's fingers dig into my shoulders a bit, and I hold my breath as fear rocks me. I pray to God that what comes out of her mouth isn't what I think it's going to be. Whatever she's about to say, it's bad.

Julie's eyebrows draw in and her lips pull into a tight line while she tries hard to fight back tears. "No. He's not."

As soon as the words leave her lips, she bursts into tears. She gasps and begins crying so hard that she can barely catch her breath.

The three of us are paralyzed, like we didn't just hear what she said.

"What do you mean? Did he get hurt?" Jared licks his lips slowly and gives her a gentle shake. When she's unable to answer him, he raises his voice, causing her to jump. "Tell me!"

"Jared . . ." she whispers, and then her gaze turns up to Wes, who is still by my side. "Wes . . . your dad . . . he's . . . he's . . ."

Jared drops his head into his hands and nearly collapses onto the floor but is able to keep his body upright. A hard sob rips through him, and he fights hard to catch his breath. Wes's hand flies to his mouth as tears begin pouring from his eyes.

My heart breaks for this family that I love so much. I don't even bother trying to hide my tears as I drop down to my knees beside Jared and attempt to wrap my arms around him to comfort him the only way I can. "Jared . . . oh my God. I'm so—"

"Don't you dare say it. Don't you dare!" The panic mixed with anger in Jared's voice is clear. "If you say it out loud, then it makes it real."

Julie bites her bottom lip and reaches out to touch Jared's shoulder. "He's gone, son."

"No!" Jared roars, leaping to his feet and knocking me back onto my butt in the process. His eyes are wide and have a wild look like I've never seen before, and it scares me a bit, but I understand why he's come unhinged. "Don't you lie to me!"

"Son . . . please," Julie pleads. "This is hard enough."

"No! You're wrong. The army's wrong. My dad . . . he's strong. He promised me he would be back. He *promised*! There's no way that he's dead! Dad wouldn't break his word like that."

I push myself up off the floor and reach out to Jared, but the moment I wrap my fingers around his biceps he shrugs me off. "Don't touch me!"

I flinch but understand his rage and jerk my hand away. Wes wraps his arm tightly around me, as if to protect me from my own boyfriend, and then pulls me back a couple steps. Wes's attempt to hold me back doesn't stop me from trying to reason with Jared.

"Jared, please." I beg for him to just take a breath and realize that he's not the only one hurting.

His eyes snap in my direction and then they zero in on Wes's hand on my shoulder. His face twists as he narrows his eyes. "Get your fucking hands off of her!"

My eyes widen as Jared directs his anger over the news we just heard onto his brother, who is only attempting to comfort me.

Wes lifts his hand off of me and then holds them both up. Wes's surrender doesn't mean anything to Jared, because he takes a step closer to his brother. Standing toe to toe, they are nearly the same height, but Jared's got about twenty pounds or so on Wes. Both men stand there in the kitchen, breathing heavily, neither backing down.

Jared stares into Wes's eyes. "Don't you ever touch her again or I swear to God—"

"Jared!" Julie jumps up from her chair, trying to stop her sons from coming to blows. "Enough! We're all upset, and we just need to calm down."

His mother's voice seems to cut through Jared's anger enough to freeze him in place. After a long moment, Jared simply shakes his head and takes a step back. "This is bullshit," he yells so loud that I swear the pictures on the walls shake. He takes yet another step back away from Wes. "I'm out of here."

"Ja—" I start to chase after him, but again Wes grabs me, locking me into place while Jared storms out of the kitchen.

The front door slams, and the distinct rumble of his truck engine roaring to life causes my breath to catch. I'm so stunned by the entire situation that my brain isn't functioning properly to alert me right away that Jared shouldn't be alone right now, no matter how angry he is and how much he wants to be on his own. He needs someone with him, and it hurts a bit that he won't let me be there for him.

I take a deep breath and decide that I'm not going to let him push me out right now.

I turn to chase after him, but Wes halts me in my tracks. "Don't, London. He needs time to process this on his own. He's too worked up right now to listen to reason. I don't want him to fly off the handle and hurt you."

My brow furrows. "He would never—"

"Not intentionally, no, but Jared isn't himself right now. You saw that. Give him space. Let him calm down," Wes says.

Julie begins crying again as the three of us remain in the kitchen together. Her soft cries fill the room, and my heart instantly begins to crumble as the realization of the situation hits me hard. While I loved Henry, I know that the love I had for him doesn't compare to the love Jared had for his father. The hardest thing I've ever had to face in my life was the death of my own mother. Life for Jared without his dad will never be the same. The same goes for Wes and Julie too.

I pull out the chair next to Julie and sit next to her, taking her hand in my own while Wes sits on the opposite side of her, mimicking my actions with her other hand.

I lick my dry lips as I choose my next words carefully. "Do you know exactly what happened to Henry?"

Wes worries his bottom lip, and I can tell he's waiting with bated breath for that answer.

I release Julie's hand and grab a napkin from the little porcelain holder sitting in the middle of the table. I hold it out to her, and she takes it and wipes her nose. "They say he was guarding a convoy when it was attacked by members of the Taliban. There were three Kuwaiti citizens and two other military policemen who were also killed. It was a routine route to transport food and water to the starving civilians who were thrown into the middle of this war. Henry jumped out of the deuce and a half to assist a wounded child and was shot through the neck."

Wes draws in a sharp breath and bites his bottom lip in an attempt to stop it from trembling, and my heart is obliterated into a million pieces.

A lump fills my throat, and my eyes burn as I picture what Henry's last few seconds on this earth must have been like. A weight sits on my chest and I gasp. It's like all the air has been sucked from the room, making it nearly impossible to breathe.

Julie takes a deep breath and then sniffs. "There was nothing they could do to save him. He died right there on the scene. I just wish I could've had the chance to tell him good-bye—to tell him how much I loved him."

I squeeze her hand. "I'm sure he never questioned that. The love you shared with him—it was so evident—so I know without a doubt you, Jared, and Wes were the last ones on his mind. He loved you all so much."

Tears continue to pour from Julie's eyes as her gaze meets mine. "Thank you, London. And I know you meant the world to him too. He always spoke about you as if you were already a part of the family. It was never a question of if you would marry our son, but when. We all love you very much."

Those sweet words only make me cry harder, and my thoughts shift to Jared. If I'm breaking this much inside, I can only imagine the pain he's going through. I wish he would allow me to be by his side to comfort him, but grief is a strange thing. Some people like me need people around them, while others like Jared need space to process what's happened.

As if Julie has read my mind, she says, "Go to him, London. He needs you right now even if he doesn't know it."

I nod and wipe my face. "Okay."

I lean in and wrap my arms around her. "I'm so sorry about Henry. I loved him like a dad."

When I pull back, she cups my face. "I know that, sweet girl, and he loved you like a daughter."

I glance over at Wes, who now has nearly the same exact vacant expression that Julie wore when we first found her sitting at this kitchen table. He's always been the more reserved brother—the one who seems to keep everything together, much like their mother—while Jared tends to be more adventurous like their father.

I push myself up from the table and then walk around to the side Wes is sitting on. I bend down and hug him, and he instantly wraps his arms around me. He buries his face in my hair and inhales deeply. "Thank you for being here."

His kind words make me feel like I belong here with this family and I'm not some intruder on this very private, heart-wrenching affair.

I rub his back while he clings to me. "I'll always be here if you guys need me."

I pull back, and Wes releases me and looks to his mother, and then back to me. "I would take you to look for Jared, but I think it's best if I stay here with Mom. I don't want to be the thing he directs his anger on, because he's obviously pissed at me right now. Promise me that you'll be careful and call me if you need me."

I nod. "I promise. I'll walk to my house and use Dad's car to drive around a bit. I know of a few places that he may have taken off to. I'll start by checking those places first."

"I mean it, London. Call me if you need anything. I'll be here for you," he says, and then his eyes soften. "Always."

The tender expression accompanied with his sweet plea for me to lean on him in this situation is very touching, and it means so much to me.

"Thank you." I place my hand on his forearm. "I promise that I will," I tell him before I turn and head out the door, on a mission to find Jared before he does something crazy.

## 11

*THEN*
**JARED**

I've been sitting at this intersection for what feels like hours. It's not busy, so I've sat here behind the wheel of my truck watching the traffic lights go through three rotations as I try to figure out where to go. It wasn't like I had an exact plan when I stormed out of my house, but I couldn't take being there for one more second. The walls were closing in around me, and I wasn't ready to hear any more details about my father being gone.

The last word echoes around in my brain: gone. That word can be used in so many contexts. Some are positive, like every cookie we brought for the bake sale is gone, while others are so bitter and vile that no one wants to hear them. My father is gone, as in forever, as in he's never coming back, and I don't understand what I'm supposed to do with that information.

There will be no more Sunday phone calls from Dad—no more working on the car together to get it running top notch. No more jamming on the guitar together. No more . . . Everything has changed. Everything is different.

I stare at the red light in front of me on display, mocking me by putting my life on hold. When it turns green again, I still haven't made up my mind where I'm going, but an angry horn blaring behind me tells me that my time just sitting here is over.

I crank the wheel to the right and mash the gas. It doesn't take long before I find myself in the shady part of Knoxville. I don't venture around here much, and soon I discover that I'm lost and have no clue where to go from here. I glance down at my gas gauge and notice that it's on empty, but luckily for me the bright lights of a station illuminate the night sky.

The tires roll over the pavement, bouncing me inside the cab as I come to a stop beside a gas pump. When I open the door, I fish my wallet from my back pocket and head toward the store to pay.

On the way in, my gaze meets the brown eyes of a tall, skinny white guy with a beanie and red flannel shirt hanging out just outside the door. The clothing choice strikes me as odd, considering it's May in Tennessee, which doesn't exactly call for dressing warm. He twitches his nose before wrinkling it, and I catch a glimpse of his toothless smile. That takes me aback because the guy can't be much older than I am, yet the roughness of his appearance gives off the impression that he's much older.

When he catches me staring, he tilts his head and lifts his eyebrows as if to silently ask me what I want. Instead, I jerk my gaze away and shove through the heavy glass door. After prepaying for the gas, I return to my truck and take another long look in the man's direction before I head back to fill my tank.

Bugs swarm the buzzing lights overhead as I set the nozzle on automatic fill and then grip the side of the truck bed and lower my head onto my arms. I sigh and wish there was some way to escape and forget about everything for a while.

My gaze snaps back up, and again I zero in on the man standing next to the building. Without really thinking about what I'm doing, I head toward the guy and leave my truck there to fill up.

When I step up in front of him, I shove my hands into my pockets. "Um, do you . . ."

Shit. I'm not even sure how to ask this.

"You lookin' to get high, homey?" His voice is deeper than I expected, and it catches me off guard.

I furrow my brow, unsure of what to say.

"You need something or not? I've got the best shit. It'll take you to a new high, man—shit so good it will make you forget your own fucking name." He rubs the tip of his nose with his index finger.

While I've never done drugs before—always on the straight and narrow because I love baseball so much—I have to admit that losing my mind for a bit sounds pretty damn perfect right now. Against my better judgment, I decide to see what he has to offer.

I nod. "Yeah, what do you have?"

The skinny man wearing a red flannel shirt smiles. "Shit, homey, I got whatever you want."

My thoughts drift over every movie I've ever seen, searching for the right terms to use, and I come up with only one way to ask for pot without seeming clueless. "Do you have a dime bag?"

He nods. "Not here, though." He points his finger in the air and then does a circle motion. "There's eyes all around. Meet me around back after you get your gas."

My pulse races under my skin, and I know how wrong this is and what it will cost me if I get caught, but I need to do this. At least with the rush of danger, I'm avoiding the real problem at hand.

The guy steps back and stuffs his hands in his pockets. "You know where I'll be."

"Sounds good." It's the only reply I can think of at the moment.

I swallow deeply, and a click alerts me to the fact that my truck is now full. I run across the empty lot and remove the nozzle, pull a fifty from my wallet, and hop into my truck. Just like he said, the guy is waiting around back, and the minute I'm close enough, he approaches.

I roll down the window and hold out the cash. "Change?"

The guy shakes his head. "I don't do change, but I'll throw in a rock."

"Fine." I should refuse it—crack is way above my speed level when it comes to this shit, but this isn't exactly like buying something from a store where they have change readily on hand. It's not like I'll use it. Besides, I'm already nervous enough, so spending any longer out here than I have to isn't a bright idea.

He rips the money from my hand and then shoves a couple baggies into it. "If you need more—"

Red-and-blue flashing lights accompanied by the distinct chirp of a police siren cause the guy to take off. A police cruiser skids to a stop and both doors fly open. One cop in a black uniform goes by the passenger side of my truck like a blur, hot on the guy's heels, while the other cop from the car approaches my truck with his gun drawn.

Oh, shit!

This cannot be fucking happening to me right now.

"Place both hands outside the truck and slowly open the door using the outside handle," the policeman orders.

The urge to duck out of this truck and run is overwhelming, but I know trying something stupid like that will only cause things to get a whole lot worse.

"All right!" I yell back as I do as he orders—both of my hands shaking uncontrollably when I stick them outside the window. "Don't shoot!"

The second my door opens, I step out. The bright headlights from the cop car shine directly into my eyes, and I use my hands to shield them. I feel like I'm on a really bad episode of *Cops*. I've always heard the saying "wrong place at the wrong time," and, shit, it's never been truer than right now.

"Keep your hands up!" he screams as he rushes over to me and grabs me by the shirt collar, shoving me down to the ground, face-first, not giving me a chance to plead my case at all.

The wind whooshes from my lungs, and the man immediately jumps on my back and shoves his knee against my spine to hold me in place. "Jesus. Do you have to be so rough? I'm fucking cooperating."

Mouthing off probably isn't a good idea, but I couldn't just allow him to treat me like a common criminal and not at least attempt to stand up for myself.

"Shut up!" he orders as he grabs my arms and jerks them behind my back before cuffing them together. The cop begins patting me down. "Do you have any knives, weapons, or needles that can poke me?"

"No, man. Nothing," I say as the taste of dirt from the ground slips into my mouth from where I'm lying, cheek down.

"What are you doing out here?" he asks after he searches me and finds nothing, but I remain quiet, not wanting to say anything that will get me into any more trouble. "Answer me!"

"Nothing!" I answer after I see that I won't be able to get away without saying anything at all.

He laughs bitterly, and if I had to guess, I would say he's rolling his eyes at me. "That's bullshit. When I search your vehicle, am I going to find anything?"

I pull my lips into a tight line. How in the fuck am I going to get out of this? The best thing I can do in this situation is come clean.

Maybe he'll let me go if he knows what I've been through this evening—if he knows that this isn't an everyday thing for me.

"I'm only going to ask you this one more time. Am I going to find anything?" he asks again with more authority ringing through his voice.

I suck in a breath and then release it through my nose. "Yes, but you have to let me explain. This is the first time I've ever done anything like this."

"That's what they all say." He reaches down and grabs my shoulder and my cuffed wrists and hoists me to my feet.

"You have to believe me, Officer. It's true," I plead.

"Why would I?" He walks me toward his squad car.

I close my eyes. I don't want to say it. I don't want to admit the truth out loud, because then it makes it real, and I'm not ready to face that. Running away from reality is the exact reason that I'm right here, right now.

The cop opens the door, and when I see the backseat, I panic. I know I have no choice but to tell him if I want any shot of getting out of this situation. "I found out that my dad died, and I was looking for something to take me out of this reality. When the guy came up to me and offered a way to forget about things, I took him up on the offer."

The officer leans me back against the car. It's the first time I'm able to get a good look at him. He's about six inches shorter than me, with a very stocky build, and his gray hair pokes out from under his hat, revealing that he's got a bit of age on him.

He frowns, and I can read a bit of sympathy in his dark eyes. "I'm really sorry to hear about your dad, but, son, the law is the law, and running to drugs isn't the way to solve your problems."

I lick my lips, and it's not like I don't already know it. Turning to them was an impulse decision that I wish I could take back. "I realize that, sir, but I obviously have a lot of shit going on right now. If you let me go, I swear to God that you'll never catch me back on this side of town again."

He shakes his head. "It doesn't work that way. If I find drugs in that truck of yours, I have to report you, and you'll have to face up to having them in your possession."

My heart races in my chest. "No, please. You don't understand. If I get caught with drugs, I'll lose my scholarship. I'll lose everything I've worked for my entire life over one stupid, rushed decision."

He furrows his brow. "Scholarship? You look familiar. What's your name?"

I lift my chin. "Jared Kraft."

Both of his eyebrows rise up. "The Volunteers baseball pitcher?"

The only answer I give him is a quick nod.

The moment I confirm who I am, his eyes grow wide. "Shit, son. I heard them talking about you on ESPN the other day. All the analysts are calling you the next big thing. Why are you of all people out here buying drugs? You've got so much to lose."

"I know that," I reply, "but like I said, I made a mistake. I just found out my father died overseas and . . . I don't know what I am. I'm not myself right now."

He sighs. "I understand. I really do, and I wish I could do something for you, but the truth of the matter is all of this has already been documented on camera." He jerks his thumb over his shoulder in the direction of the squad car. "And besides that, if my partner catches the dealer, we'll have no choice but to take him downtown. We can't allow riffraff like that to run the streets and sell to teenagers and be the cause of someone's death. I'm sorry, Jared, but my hands are tied."

"Shit," I mutter and tip my head up to the sky.

If Dad is watching this right now, I know he's fucking pissed at me. I've let him down. I've let my family down, and more importantly

I've let myself down. I ran out on my mother and brother when I know they needed me to be there and be strong, but I broke down like a coward—unable to face the harsh reality of the truth—and left them. How could I have done that? I hate letting people down. My integrity is one thing I prize, and I've lost it in one night. How can the people I love ever trust me to stick by them in the future when things get tough? And now, with this drug thing, it'll destroy everything. My future—London's future with me—may all be shot to shit after this.

I treated London so cold before I walked out the door tonight. She probably won't forgive me. I know I wouldn't if I were her. The way I lashed out at her—I've never done that before. I didn't even know that part of me existed, and to be honest, with how fucked up my head is right now, I can't promise that I'll never do it again. I can't control this anger inside me, and the last thing in the world I want to do is hurt her. I already hate myself right now for how I just treated her. If things keep going like this, I may not be the best thing for her anymore.

## NOW
## JARED

**W**e've been on the road for a couple of months now in support of our second album. It's one of the hottest days of the year, and Wicked White is one of the headlining bands for Summerfest. We've worked really hard to get to this point, not to mention our struggles with one another in order to make it to the big league.

Jane Ann rushes past me without giving me a single glance, her bright red hair swishing around as she frantically whips her head back and forth as if she's looking for something.

I lift one eyebrow when she finally spots me and then makes a beeline toward me. "Looking for someone?"

She twists her red lips. "Yes, you. Where are Luke and Tyler? I need to speak with all of you."

I shrug. "How should I know? I'm not their babysitter."

Jane Ann crosses her arms over her chest. "Attitude like that is exactly what I need to speak with all of you about."

"Really? I happen to believe that there's not one thing wrong with my attitude," I retort. "My contract doesn't mention anything about me being fucking rainbows and sunshine. It says that I'm to show up, do my job, and that's it, and I assure you I've never missed a show. Hell, if I had a time card, I'd be employee of the year with perfect attendance."

Her face flushes, and I can tell she's ready to rip into me but is trying hard to maintain her composure since there are so many people milling about around us in the backstage area. "Jared, you need to learn to respect others. This mouth of yours causes nothing but trouble."

I roll my eyes. "Respect others? Like who?"

"Ace, for one."

That causes a bitter laugh to tear out of me. "Ace? Are you fucking kidding me? Why should I respect him?"

She straightens her back. "Because after tonight I'm making him your boss. I'm putting him in charge of this band, giving him more authority to make minor calls to keep him happy, so you better get used to biting your tongue when it comes to Ace." She glances down at her watch, and I open my mouth to fire back, but she cuts me off. "Speaking of which, Ace has a signing appearance to make, but I expect all of you to be waiting side stage to take direction from Ace as soon as he's done signing autographs. If you're late, for anything, you will be fined. Make sure you find the other two and let them know."

She walks off, twisting her hips in her too-tight red skirt in the process.

"I wonder how big the stick up her ass is? Fucker must be huge for her to be a constant bitch." Luke's voice pulls me out of the trance I was in watching Jane Ann walk away.

God, that woman and her little pet, Ace, get under my skin.

"What did she want this time?" My gaze turns to my redheaded bandmate who stands beside Tyler, the dirty-blond-haired drummer. Both of the men stare at me, waiting on my answer.

I rub the back of my neck. "She came to tell me that I have a bad attitude and that we better start showing Ace more respect. Oh, and she's also imposing fines if we're late."

Tyler's green eyes widen. "Respect him? Is she kidding me?"

"Afraid not. She told me to make sure we are waiting side stage for Ace because she plans on making him our boss," I inform them.

"Our boss?" Luke says so loud he might as well shout it from the rooftop. "Now I know that bitch has lost her mind. They might've been able to make Ace the face of the band, but I'll never follow his lead without a fight. It's bad enough he tries to order us around every chance he gets when it comes to the way we play."

I understand their anger because I share in their feelings, but I'm not sure how much we can actually fight the change. From now on, it looks as though Ace will pretty much own us, and I hate that. I hate the idea of being at his disposal.

We sit backstage together, waiting for Ace to show up. I find it funny that Wicked White was scheduled for an autograph session with the fans, and yet most of the band isn't there. Only Ace. It's complete bullshit how we get treated like Ace's backup, but it's becoming clear to me that's exactly what we are.

An hour later, I spot Jane Ann making her way toward us with Ace by her side. Ace looks up and catches me staring at him, and it takes every muscle in my body to remain calm and not tell his ass off.

"I'm glad all you guys are here on time," Jane Ann says as she approaches Tyler, Luke, and me. "I see my little warning of imposing fines for tardiness has made a difference."

"Not all of us have you as our personal fucking wristwatch." Tyler's tone makes it clear that he's not happy, but that doesn't faze our bitchy manager. He shoves a piece of his hair out of his eyes. "Why don't the rest of us get the same coddling that Ace gets? You always take it easy on him."

Luke glances over at me and smirks before releasing a small laugh. He absolutely loves it when our normally quiet Tyler spouts off at the mouth. He doesn't say much, but when he's mad, he's direct. Sugarcoating things isn't in Tyler's nature, and sometimes I'm glad that he speaks up. It's nice that I'm not the only one showing my utter disdain for the entire situation.

Ace studies us, and the expression on his face tells me that he'd like nothing more than for us all to go to hell, but he doesn't have the balls to tell us that. Besides, he knows just as well as anyone that he gets treated far better than we do. I mean, the guy would have to be a fucking moron if he didn't realize it.

I sigh heavily. If Jane Ann wants me to treat Ace like he's above me, I might as well start treating him like he's royalty. "So what's our set list like for tonight, Your Highness?"

Ace's nostrils flare, and I love that I'm getting to him. Why should he get it so easy? He hasn't done anything better than we have, and I certainly don't think he's more talented that any of us—namely me.

"Same set as last night, but we'll be canceling the next couple of shows on the tour," Ace says, like him making the decision to cancel a few shows is no big deal.

"What?!" Now the douche bag is messing with my money. That shit isn't going to fly.

Ace flinches as his gaze whips between Jane Ann and me. It's like he's in shock that we'd be pissed over this.

"What the fuck do you mean we're canceling?" Luke asks, his fiery tone matching the color of his hair. "We've booked enough dates to be set for a long time. We can't go canceling shit now."

"Look, guys, I'm sorry, but my mother is sick—"

Oh, I have to stop this fucker right there. I know for a fact that's a lie. How dare he use an excuse like that when it's a known fact he grew up in the system.

"That's horseshit. You don't even have a mother. You were a fucking orphan."

He narrows his eyes, and it's obvious that he doesn't like being called out on his bullshit.

"Shut your damn mouth before I shut it for you," Ace fires back at me, which only pisses me off further.

I don't take threats well. My pulse races as I take a step closer to Ace, closing the distance between us. I've got him by at least two inches and probably twenty-five or so pounds. Ace doesn't work out like I do. It's clear from his puny muscles. I lock my gaze onto his and dare him to hit me, begging him to give me a reason to fuck him up.

Ace's toe bumps into mine, and I'm instantly taken aback by his bravery to stand up to me. He usually just storms off and sulks, avoiding confrontation. It still doesn't change the fact that I will end him if he tests me, because he doesn't scare me one damn bit.

Ace looks directly into my eyes. "That sounds like a threat."

"You bet your ass it is," I reply coolly.

Jane Ann wedges her petite frame between us. This is her worst nightmare realized: someone like me who has already been chomping at the bit to get my hands on this guy and prove he isn't all that. "Both of you knock this shit off right now. I won't tolerate physical violence of any kind. This isn't going to happen if you want to stay on Mopar's payroll."

Jane Ann knows that's the one thing that will reel me back in— the money. I have nothing else in my life but music, and I'm pretty damn lucky to be able to make a living doing it, so I don't want to fuck that up.

I take a step back and raise my hands in surrender. "Fine. Just keep Boy Wonder here out of my face."

That hits a nerve, because Ace tenses, and Jane Ann shoves her hand into his chest to keep him from lunging forward. "Cool it, Ace. This is neither the time nor place." She turns back around to face us with one of the meanest scowls I've ever seen. "You three, go wait side stage."

Luke rolls his eyes, and Tyler stalks off toward the stage with drumsticks in hand—both doing what they were told. Before I go, I overhear Jane Ann scold Ace for telling us that he's canceling shows. Seems as though he doesn't have as much authority as he thought.

That last little bit causes me to smile as I pick up my guitar.

"Wicked White. You're up," the stage manager for Summerfest tells the three of us. "Go ahead and take the stage."

I turn back to where we left Jane Ann and Ace. Jane Ann is throwing her hands around wildly, and Ace is leaning forward, pointing his finger at her. Looks like things aren't so rosy on the other side of the fence right now.

Tyler is the first to walk out on stage, and the crowd goes insane while Luke and I follow.

We stand on stage with the fans chanting "Wicked White," and I glance back at the other two guys and shrug. It's not like Ace to keep fans waiting. He knows that's bad for business, and Jane Ann certainly does, but from the looks of it, Ace is having second thoughts about performing. It appears that he doesn't want to come on stage, and Jane Ann is physically shoving him in our direction.

Ace's jaw hangs open like he's shocked that Jane Ann just forced him out here. He continues to stare at her as if he's trying to process exactly what has just gone down.

I nod at Tyler and Luke, and we all begin to play, hoping to get this show on the road so we don't look clueless in front of the crowd. Tyler taps out the opening song—which is the same one we opened with last night, just like Ace wants. The three of us look to one another because Ace misses his cue to start singing. The fucker hasn't even picked up the mic yet.

What in the hell is he doing? Is he trying to make us all look like dumbasses who don't know what we're doing? I think he's doing this shit on purpose over the little exchange we had only moments ago.

Finally, Ace turns to face us. He takes the time to stare at each one of us individually with an unreadable face. I knew the guy was an asshole, but now we can add certifiably insane after this show. No wonder Jane Ann gives him his way most of the time.

When he points his gaze on me, his brow furrows like he's trying to figure me out, and then he jams his fingers into his bronze hair.

I stand still on the stage but continue to play, hoping that whatever it is he's going through, he figures this shit out fast. In front of a sold-out festival isn't the time or place to have a breakdown of some sort.

He squeezes his eyes shut and then opens them to stare at us while we wait on him to sing. Ace raises both of his hands and flips his middle finger in our direction before he turns on his heel and storms off stage without uttering a single word.

Jane Ann's jaw drops as he stalks past her, completely ignoring her orders to get back on stage.

With wide eyes I watch as our band's front man walks away from everything he's worked for, and in an odd way, I relate to him.

## NOW
## LONDON

I stare, lost in thought, at the box of chocolates from Julie's shop, which sits next to a dozen roses on my desk. Today was exhausting, and all I want to do is go home and put my feet up. A glass of wine thrown in there wouldn't hurt. The kids were really hyper in class today for some reason, and it makes me wonder if tonight will be a full moon or something.

Peyton's little voice singing "The Wheels on the Bus" while he draws a picture with crayons pulls me out of the trance.

I push myself up from my desk and walk around behind him. He's drawn a picture of himself holding hands with his mom and dad while baby Brody stands in front of him. Stick people drawings by children are the best. They speak volumes about what the child is feeling.

"That's really good, Peyton," I tell him.

"Thank you," he replies as he begins adding another stick figure to the picture.

"Who are you adding in there?" I ask, curious as to who else he pictures in his family.

"You," he tells me but stays hard at work.

"Me?" I ask, completely surprised. "Why are you adding me to your family picture?"

He stares up at me with his hazel eyes. "Mommy says you don't have your own family, so I'm making you a part of ours because you and Mommy are friends."

Warmth envelops my heart and I smile. The sweet words from this small boy truly touch me. Sam is certainly raising this little guy right by teaching him to care about others.

I pull out the chair next to him and sit down as we wait for Sam to show up. "That's very nice of you, Peyton. I really appreciate that."

"You're welcome," he says as he draws a purple dress on the stick figure that's supposed to represent me. He grows quiet for a minute, but then he looks up at me. "Mrs. Kraft, will you always be sad?"

I chew on the inside of my lower lip. "Who said I was sad?"

"Mommy. I heard her tell Daddy on the phone that you were still sad. I figured if I made you a part of my family you wouldn't be sad anymore."

I squat down beside him and pat his little arm. "You are such a sweet kid, and you know what else? I would love to be a part of your family. I already think of your mommy as my sister."

That makes him smile. "Good. I'm glad I've made you not sad now."

Peyton happily returns to coloring his picture, and I wish with all my might that it could only be so simple to not be sad anymore. If there was some sort of switch to instantly turn off heartbreak, I would've used that a long time ago.

Maybe it is time to let Jared go. If even a kid can see that I'm sad, I'm not doing a very good job of hiding it.

I have to find a way to let go.

"You probably hate me for always making you late, huh?"

I glance up to find Sam walking into my classroom, holding Brody.

"Stop being ridiculous. It's impossible to be mad at you." I push myself up to my feet. "How was your day?"

"Ugh. Long, but I didn't get thrown up on, so that's always a good day in my book." She smiles.

I laugh, and even though I don't have any children of my own, I can fully relate, seeing as how I have a classroom full of little ones who tend to get sick a lot. "Agreed."

Sam adjusts Brody on her hip as he twirls her necklace around his chubby little fingers before she points to my desk. "More gifts?"

I nod. "It's the fifth arrangement this week, and if he keeps sending all the candy, I'll weigh five million pounds before long."

She shakes her head. "I'll say one thing for Wes, he makes it impossible for you to not think about him, even when the two of you are on a break."

I run my fingers through my dark hair. "We might as well not be on a break as much as he texts and sends me things."

"Give the guy a break," Sam says. "He doesn't want to lose you after how much work he put in to get you in the first place."

I furrow my brow. "You think he put in that much effort after . . . well, after what happened?"

Sam tilts her head and gives me the "you've got to be kidding me" face. "London, I've never seen a man put in that much work to land a girl. The guy spent nearly four years being your shoulder to cry on after his asshole brother left you without so much as a good-bye. I would call that a mammoth undertaking. No man works that hard for nothing."

"That's what sucks about this whole situation. I feel like such a"—I mouth the word "bitch" to Sam to avoid little ears overhearing—"for putting him through all this. I wish I could love him back the way he seems to love me."

"Aww, Mommy said a dirty word," Peyton chimes in.

"It's okay, Peyt. Adults are allowed to say them if they want," Sam tells him.

I can see the little wheels turning in his brain. "So when I become a man, I can say them too?"

I cover my mouth to hide my snicker, and Sam immediately smacks my arm in response before addressing his question. "Yes. When you become a grown-up, you can say whatever words you want."

Peyton's little hand draws into a fist, and he draws his elbow back to do a fist pump. "All right! I can't wait to be a man."

Sam rolls her eyes. "Lord help me when he gets older. I'm going to be in so much trouble. Josh will not be allowed to remain in the service once these two become teens. I'll need him around to help me wrangle them in."

I nod. "You'll most definitely have your hands full."

"Okay, Peyton, get your book bag," Sam orders and then turns to me. "Want to go grab an early dinner with me and the boys? I so don't feel like cooking today."

I smile, loving the fact that I really do feel like a part of their family.

## THEN
## LONDON

All night long, I comb the streets of Knoxville, desperate to find
Jared. Clearly he's not in the right frame of mind, and I don't
want him to get hurt. I've visited every possible place where Jared
might be. I even went to our old high school on the off chance that
he might be there running the track like he used to do back in the
day when he got upset over something.

Jared isn't hotheaded. I've never seen him blow up like the way
he did tonight, but it's not like I can fault him for it. How a person
reacts to the news of the death of someone they love is a very indi-
vidual thing.

When my mother died, I was devastated, but I kept most of my
emotions to myself. I wasn't able to hide the tears at times, but just
how much I missed her was something I rarely spoke about with
anyone.

Time is what Jared needs to heal. When something bothers him,
he usually throws himself into baseball—training harder and putting in longer hours in the gym. It's like playing baseball is his form

of meditation—a place where he can mull over all the things that bother him.

I turn back into our subdivision, and part of me fully expects Jared's truck to be parked in his mother's driveway, but sadly, he's still missing.

I worry my bottom lip back and forth between my teeth as I park the car. The headlights shining through the living room windows must've caught Wes's attention, because before I've even had a chance to get out of the car, he is opening the front door.

His blond hair is a disheveled mess, like he's run his fingers through it over and over, something I've noticed he does when he's anxious. The second his brown eyes scan my face, he frowns. I know the expression on my face is one showing nothing but disappointment. "No luck?"

I shake my head. "I've checked everywhere I can think of, and I didn't find a sign of him."

Wes sighs. "He's so selfish. I'm pretty pissed at him for making Mom worry about him. She doesn't need this right now. She's already going through hell."

He's right. Julie doesn't need to be here worrying about Jared. I understand he's hurting, but so are his mom and brother—and even me. I haven't even really had time to sit down and process my own emotions because I've been so wrapped up in how Jared feels.

"I'm sure he'll turn up," I reassure Wes. "He just needs some time."

Wes glances back to the door. "Do you want to come in and wait? I made some tea for Mom while you were gone, and there's enough for a few more cups."

"That sounds nice. Thank you."

He gives me a tight-lipped smile. "Anytime, London."

When I step up beside him, he wraps his arm around my shoulders and leads me into the house.

The rest of the night goes by, and I'm not sure which of the three of us paces the most as we wait anxiously for Jared's return. Once he gets back, after I know he's safe, I'm going to give him an earful for causing everyone so much worry.

By five in the morning there's still no sign of Jared, and Julie's worry is now bordering on panic. "This isn't like him. My Jared is not this irresponsible."

"He probably went out and picked up a bottle of Jack and drank until he passed out somewhere," Wes says. "We're probably worried for nothing."

"Well, he wasn't in his dorm, and every friend that I know of back at school hadn't seen him. If he drank, he did it alone," I tell Wes.

Julie rubs her face. "Maybe I should start calling the hospitals. He could be hurt. I know the police won't take reports until an adult has been missing for a couple days."

Wes shakes his head. "I doubt anything like that's happened, but if it makes you feel better, Mom, I'll help you make some calls."

I sit on the couch, chewing my thumbnail while Wes and Julie get to work making phone calls. Just as Wes suspected, Jared isn't listed at any hospital facility, which is a relief.

When seven rolls around, I find myself so exhausted that I doze off sitting straight up on their living room couch. I jump the moment someone touches me, and my eyes snap open to find Wes tucking a blanket around me.

"You are so nice. I should be taking care of you right now, and not the other way around," I say sleepily, knowing he's the one who just lost his father.

Wes's brown eyes trace over my face. "No. You're exhausted. Try and get some rest. I'll wake you up when he comes home."

"Okay," I answer, too tired to get much more out before I fall back asleep.

The shrill ring of a telephone awakens me, and I tear my eyes open. I'm not sure how long I've been out, but it's long enough that I have a tiny spot of drool on the side of my face.

Wes shoves himself up from the chair across from me and grabs the house phone. "Hello?"

The moment he answers, his eyebrows draw in and a confused look crosses his face.

I yank the blanket off of me and sit up a little straighter just as Julie rounds the corner with a dish towel in her hands.

"Yes. I'll accept," Wes says to the other person on the line.

Julie wrings the towel in her hands. "Who is it?"

Wes holds up an index finger. "Jared, where the hell are you?"

I scoot to the edge of my seat as I wait with bated breath.

"Yeah." Wes rubs the back of my neck. "We'll be down there as soon as we can. Sit tight." He nods, like he's answering a question that Jared's asked on the other end. "Don't worry about it. We'll talk when we get down there."

The moment he hangs up the phone, Julie rushes to Wes's side. "What did he say? Where is he? And why is he calling collect?"

Wes holds up his hands. "Easy, Mom. Jared is fine, but the bad news is that he got arrested last night."

"Arrested?!" Julie and I both say in unison.

Jail is the last place I ever expected to find Jared. He's too strait-laced and too focused on baseball to do anything crazy enough to land himself in jail.

"What for?" I ask.

Julie shakes her head. "I can't believe this. Jared's never been in any trouble before. What on earth could he have possibly done?"

"Drugs," Wes says simply. "They picked him up when he was buying weed."

My hand instantly covers my mouth. "Oh my God. This could be—"

"Bad. I know," Wes finishes my sentence for me. "When school finds out about this, they will most likely take away his scholarship and kick him off the team."

My eyes widen. "No! That can't happen! That will crush him."

My emotions teeter on the edge and they are millimeters from falling over. I'm mere seconds away from losing my head. If Jared loses baseball, I . . . I don't even want to think about what he'll do. He's already got enough to deal with. This will only make things ten times worse.

Julie sits down beside me and wraps her arms around me. "My boy needs you to be strong for him. He's suffering so much, and it looks like things are about to get a whole lot worse before they get better. You have to be strong."

"I'll try." I wipe my face with the back of my hand, but the tears continue to spill from my eyes.

We don't waste any time. We pile into Julie's car with Wes behind the wheel and race down to the local police station to figure out how to get Jared out of this mess if we can. The ride is quiet for the most part—none of us wanting to speculate too much on Jared's fate until we've gotten to the bottom of everything and figured out the best way to help him.

Wes pulls into the parking lot and then stops. "Here we are."

When I exit the car, my hands shake. I don't know why I'm so nervous, but I guess maybe it's the idea of knowing that everything in Jared's life is about to change. It baffles me as to what would possess him to buy drugs. For as long as I've known him, he's never touched the stuff because he was so into sports and keeping his body fit. Doing drugs was not something he was even remotely interested in.

It hurts to know that Jared felt like he had to go buy drugs in order to find comfort instead of seeking me out for it. I always thought I was his place of comfort—the person he can always turn to when he's in trouble.

Inside the building everything seems very sterile and minimal. The cinder-block walls are white and completely bare with the exception of some golden plaque honoring an officer who was killed in the line of duty. Two wooden benches sit back to back in the middle of the room, and to the right is a desk separated from us by what I imagine is bulletproof glass.

Wes explains to the small black woman in a police uniform sitting at the desk who we are there to pick up.

She nods and then presses a button in order to speak through the little speaker that's mounted on the glass. "Bail is set for fifteen hundred dollars, and he's scheduled for arraignment on May twentieth at eight in the morning."

Julie opens her purse and pulls out the wad of cash we stopped at her candy shop to get. She counts out the money before stepping up to the glass and placing it into the metal box on the counter so the female officer can pull it through to her side of the glass. Julie stuffs her wallet back into her purse as the officer sends a form through for her to fill out.

Once everything is complete, the woman tells us to have a seat while they bring Jared out.

I can't imagine being trapped in this place. This visit alone is enough to scare me straight to the point where I never want to do anything that will risk my freedom.

It takes about an hour, but a loud buzzer sounds just before the dark gray steel door rolls open on the track. A few inches separate the wall and the door as it continues to slowly open and I spot Jared. His dark hair is disheveled and his normally bright blue eyes seem dull. A glimmer of a smile passes across his face the moment he spots me, and I can tell he's happy that I'm here but is doing his best not to seem overly excited that he's getting out of this place.

I don't give him any choice. I step over to him and wrap my arms around his neck. "I was so worried. Don't you ever leave me like that again."

Strong arms wrap around my waist and pull me tighter against his chest. He buries his face in my hair and inhales deeply. "I'm sorry, London. I fucked up so bad."

I shake my head. "Shhh. Don't talk about that right now. Whatever happens, we'll figure it out."

Jared gives me one final squeeze and then releases me. When I step back and straighten my shirt, Jared looks down at his mom and frowns. "Mom . . . I'm—"

Julie wraps him in a hug. "It's okay, son. It's okay."

Once he's in his mother's comforting arms, a sob rips out of his chest. Tears that I'm sure he's been fighting since he heard the news last night about his father flow freely down his face. I glance over at Wes, who also bats away the tears from his eyes and throws his arms around both his mom and brother. Finally, they are able to grieve together over the loss of the man who was the rock of their family—the man who held them all together. It's then it hits me like a ton of bricks that life for this family will never be the same, and my heart breaks for these people that I love so much.

### NOW
### JARED

I'm still standing there in shock. I can't believe that asshole just flipped us off and then stormed off the stage like that. Ace is one selfish bastard to leave us to deal with the aftermath of an angry sold-out crowd who obviously will not be getting the show that they paid for.

There's no other choice but to cut the music and follow Ace's lead off the stage. Luke and Tyler take off first, while I'm right on their heels. The fans at Summerfest instantly boo. I turn back and watch as our instruments get pounded with half-empty beer bottles and anything else the people can find to throw onto the stage to show their protest.

"Fuck," Luke says, standing next to me. "They're pissed."

"Wouldn't you be? I mean, shit, they paid for a show, and we just walked off stage," Tyler adds.

"What choice did that asshole give us? I mean, who does that?" Luke's face is just as red as his hair.

We stand there, completely unsure of what to do next. I've never had anything like this happen before. Hopefully Jane Ann has tracked Ace down and talked some sense into that moron. He needs to get his stupid ass back on this stage before these people riot and tear this place apart.

After close to twenty minutes since Ace's Houdini act, Tyler looks to me. "Do you think he's coming back?"

I shrug. "I have no idea, but I still expect to get paid for this show. I showed up. It's not my fault Ace picked now to be a fucking diva."

No sooner do the words leave my lips than Jane Ann shows up without Ace. Her red hair is frizzy and completely disheveled. I can tell by the wild look in her blue eyes that she's losing her shit right now.

I straighten my back. "I'm going to guess that Ace told you to piss off."

She narrows her eyes at me. "It seems that Ace will not be doing the show tonight."

"Thanks for that one, Captain Obvious," Luke spouts off. "Does he plan on making the next show tomorrow night?"

Jane Ann squares her shoulders. "I'm unable to answer that at this current time. I guess we will just wait and see when we get there tomorrow."

I release a bitter laugh. "Are you fucking joking? There's no way I'm going to stand up thousands of people again. Either he's going to be there or he isn't, which is it?"

"I don't know," she answers.

"What do you mean *you don't know?*"

"It means I don't even know where he is, okay?" she growls at me. "He's gone and I have no clue where he is. He's not answering his phone—nothing—so like I said, we won't know if he's going to show up until we get to the arena tomorrow."

I pinch the bridge of my nose. "This is fucking ridiculous. I told you that you put all your eggs in the wrong basket. Guys like Ace can't handle the pressure of being center stage."

"I don't need this right now, JJ. What we need to focus on is finding Ace. His foster mother is ill, so I'm pretty sure he's heading to Ohio to see her. If any of you speak with him before I do, you better tell me, and let Ace know that I expect him to be at that show tomorrow night."

"Why would you even think that we'd talk to him before you? He rarely speaks to us, and we are definitely not his friends," I tell her. "This isn't anything new."

"Unbelievable. Well, you all better hope that we find him or we'll all be out of jobs." She doesn't give us time to say anything else, just turns on her heel and walks away.

Damn that Ace. Now he's really gone and fucked us all.

The next show comes and there's still no sign of Ace. From the information that Jane Ann was able to dig up, the woman who raised Ace passed away last night in a hospital in Columbus, Ohio. Ace was there when she died, and it's assumed that we're going to have to cancel the next few shows to give him a chance to grieve the loss and attend her funeral.

As for the rest of us, we're stuck in limbo, waiting to see when Ace will return. Jane Ann has made several attempts to reach Ace, but all of her calls have gone unanswered.

I've been cooped up in my hotel room for days, which isn't a good thing for me. It allows me too much time for my mind to wander and dwell on people in my past. The one person who's been on my mind since the day I found out that Ace's foster mother passed is my own mother.

Seeing what Ace is going through and how that shit's being publicized in the tabloids actually makes me feel sorry for him. I know firsthand how much it hurts to lose a parent, so I can sympathize with what he's going through. It also reminds me that life is precious and that there are no do-overs when it comes to people you love dying.

I haven't seen my mom in nearly five years, but she's the only one I've remained in contact with from my old life. My calls home are sporadic and short, but it's nice to know that she's okay. As much as I love Mom, it hurts too much to speak with her because I can't stop myself from thinking of Dad when I do. But it's times like these when I just need to hear the sound of her voice.

I grab my cell off the nightstand and dial the number to Mom's candy shop, where she answers on the third ring. "Best Candies."

I lick my dry lips. "Hey, Mom."

"Jared." The way she says my name it nearly sounds like a sigh of relief. She does that every time I call, like she's been waiting since the last time we spoke to see if I would call again. "It's so good to hear your voice. How are you?"

"I'm good. Busy, but good."

"Being busy is always good. It tends to keep your mind occupied," she says.

I know there's so much more she wants to say to me, but she's learned over the past few years that if she starts digging too much, or mentions London, those are the triggers that cause me to hang up. That completely makes me feel like an asshole. My life shouldn't be this way, but it is. It's royally screwed up, and I'm too much of a coward to face all the people that I've caused so much pain.

"I've heard your band mentioned a lot. What's going on with your bandmate? Looks like he flipped out during a performance," Mom says, bringing me out of my thoughts.

I sigh. "Apparently his foster mother was in the hospital, and he took off to see her. It was honestly a good thing he walked off stage, because he went right to her and was able to tell her good-bye before she passed."

Mom's quiet for a few minutes. "Not everyone is so lucky."

I swallow down the lump in my throat. I wish to God that I would've gotten a chance to see Dad and talk to him one last time. There were so many things that I wanted to say to him—tell him how much I loved him and what he meant to me—but I never got the chance. Ace is lucky, and he should count his blessings that he was so fortunate.

"Does this mean the band will be taking some time off?" she asks. "I would love for you to come home. I know Wes would—"

"Wait," I interrupt her. "Does he know we've kept in contact all this time?"

"Of course not. I haven't told anyone like you asked. I know there's some bad blood there, and that's between the two of you, although I wish you'd come home and work things out with him. He's the only family that you've got left other than me, and I would like to see the two of you become close again."

I pinch the bridge of my nose. "Wes will never forgive me for what I did. We both know that. He said so himself."

"You might be surprised at how things change over time. If you never try to make amends, how do you know what another person is willing to forgive?"

I sit on the edge of my bed, and my eyes drift up to the ceiling. Tears attempt to push their way through, but I fight like hell to stay strong and not allow my emotions to overtake me.

Am I sorry for what went down the last night I saw Wes and London? Absolutely. Can I take back what I did? No, but I wish to God that I could. I never meant for things to get out of control, and I will never forgive myself for what I did, so how can either of them?

Leaving everything behind was the best thing I could do. It was the only way that I knew to force myself out of their lives—by not being around them, not giving them a chance to forgive me.

It took me at least a year and a half before I could even call my own mother on the phone after what I did on the day the University of Tennessee decided to revoke my scholarship. I'm so ashamed of myself for everything that happened between London, Wes, and me after the school took what little bit of normalcy I had left—not to mention wrecked all the plans I had for my life—away from me.

I didn't think it was possible for my mother to love me anymore after that, but I was wrong.

"Will you think about it?" Mom asks.

"What?" I ask.

"Coming home. If you'll have time off, please consider it. I would love to see you."

I take a deep breath. I've missed her so much, and I would love the chance to see her. Life is way too short, and I need to stop being such a coward and take the risk of seeing people that I'm not exactly ready to face just yet in order to see Mom. She means the world to me, so I'll risk facing London and Wes again if I have to, although I would prefer to take baby steps and just start out by seeing Mom alone first on this visit.

"Okay, but it'll be quick, and you're the only person I want to see," I tell her.

"Of course, son. Whatever you want." I don't have to see her face to know that she's smiling.

When the plane touches down, I stare out the window at the familiar surroundings that I haven't seen in so long. We've played a couple shows in Knoxville, but I make it a point to not stick around the city long for fear of running into people that I may know. I wasn't ready to face it—not that I'm ready now, but the need to see Mom helps me overcome the fear a bit.

The captain turns off his seat belt sign, and I stand up from my aisle seat to grab the carry-on bag I brought with me. I only have one bag since I don't plan on staying long.

After trekking through the terminal to find the rental car desk, I quickly pay for my vehicle and head out down the road. Not much has changed since I've been to my hometown, but the city has gotten a few new restaurants.

The clock on the dashboard reads 2:54, and I know Mom is probably still hard at work at the shop, so I cut down Main Street and head in that direction.

Since Dad's death, Mom has thrown her entire life into this shop. She was always busy before, but since Dad's not around, the shop provides her sole income. The army provided her with some sort of death benefit money too, but I know she tries not to touch it so she has some kind of retirement.

It eases my mind a bit to know she's able to focus on something else besides having to face life without Dad around. Music was that for me. It was the only thing other than baseball that I was ever very good at.

The quiet little candy shop's windows are covered with an array of pictures displaying all the different kinds of treats she can make. I study the windows and think back on how bare they used to be. Seems Mom has livened up the place to draw customers in.

I park the Ford sedan rental and cut the engine. Part of me itches to run inside and throw my arms around Mom and pretend that the last few years never happened, while the rest of me knows there's no forgetting what's been done. For so long I lived in a fog of pain and anger. It took me a long time to wake up and realize all the damage I caused by my actions, and by then too much time had gone by. I figure it won't do any good to apologize now. I'm sure they've moved on, and bringing it up again will only reopen old wounds—wounds that I plan on leaving to heal by staying as far away from London and Wes as I can.

I take a deep breath and say a little prayer as I open the door and head out to face my past.

## THEN
## LONDON

I pick at the frayed string hanging off the corner of my purse as I sit in the lobby of the dean's office. On the other side of the thick wooden door, Jared sits in a meeting with all the bigwigs of the University of Tennessee, learning the fate of his future at this school. Getting charged with possession was only the beginning of all the crap Jared has to face. Once he went to court, they assigned him three days of community service, which he did without complaint, and gave him a twenty-five-hundred-dollar fine. Julie paid the fine, so the only thing left to do is see what the school is going to do. He was already suspended for the rest of the season, ruining any chance he had to go into the draft like he wanted to this year.

Jared's had it rough, and all of this has made grieving the loss of his father very difficult for him. He's been different since the night he found out about Henry's death—more anxious—which is understandable, because it was also the night his future went into limbo. He's become angry and bitter and isn't the same guy I've known most of my life, but I'm holding out hope that he's going to make it through all of this.

Once they tell him where he stands with his scholarship, I pray that he'll be able to get himself back on track. From everyone we've talked to, it doesn't look like he'll get in major trouble—maybe the suspension for the rest of this year will be punishment enough. It will only delay his plans for a little while because it will force him to stay another year in college-level ball to prove that he's still worth picking up as a pro.

A muffled shout from behind the door draws my attention. I'm not 100 percent sure, but it sounded like Jared's voice.

My right leg bounces of its own accord, and I chew on my thumbnail.

Shit.

Whatever is being said in there doesn't seem to be going well.

The door flies open and Jared comes tearing out of the room and passes right by me. My head whips toward the room. I notice not one person is attempting to stop him.

My heart races as I shove myself out of the chair and tear out of the building after him. He's nearly to the parking lot, so I run to catch up with him.

He reaches his truck and hops inside, and I panic that he's about to leave me behind. I run around to the passenger side and jerk the door open and jump inside just as the V-8 engine roars to life.

"What happened?" I ask, completely out of breath as he throws the truck into drive without even looking at me. I grab the door handle as he rounds the corner and squeals the tires. "Whoa. Shit. Jared, slow down!"

My order doesn't even faze him. If anything it only makes him press the gas harder and send us shrieking through the city streets well past the legal speed limit.

"Jared, please," I beg as he passes a car on a double yellow line. "Talk to me."

His head snaps in my direction, and there's a crazy-wild look in his eye unlike anything I've ever seen before. "Why?" he asks. "Do you need me to tell you myself that they yanked my scholarship away? That they kicked me off the fucking team? You're smarter than that, London. You already know why I'm so pissed."

"Can't we fix it?" There has to be a way we can make things better, or at least figure out a new route for his career path. Jared's far too great at baseball for some minor team to not give him another chance to try out as a walk-on or something.

"No, Ms. Fix-It, we can't!" he shouts. "Sometimes people fuck shit up so bad that there's no undoing what's been done, so stop trying to be like your father and fix things."

"But—" I open my mouth to tell him that there has to be something that we can do, but I'm immediately cut off.

"Just shut up!"

I raise my eyebrows and my mouth falls open. He's never spoken to me like that before, so it catches me off guard. It's like the Jared I've known all these years is slowly disappearing, and this new, enraged version of him is taking over.

I bite my bottom lip when it begins to quiver and turn my head away. I can't even look at him right now, because if I do, I know I'll burst into tears, and judging from his mood, that's the last thing he needs from me right now. Tears in this instance won't solve anything.

We don't say another word to one another for the rest of the ride home. I stay on the opposite side of the truck away from him and don't dare to slide over into my normal place next to him on the bench seat. It doesn't feel like a spot I'd be very welcomed in right now anyhow.

Jared skids to a stop in front of my house. I glance over at him, and he sits there looking straight ahead, not even so much as glancing in my direction. The anger I get. Being pissed off that his scholarship was yanked away over an irresponsible, impulsive act I completely understand too. But what I don't get is why he's taking his anger out on me. All I want to do is help him. I don't know why he can't see that.

"Jared . . ." I say, hoping that my voice, pleading his name, will help him get through whatever anger cloud surrounds his rational mind to let him know that, no matter what, I still care about him and love him.

"Get out, London. This, for once, isn't about you, so don't make it out to be like it is. I'm not going to talk about how I'm completely falling short on everything I planned to do—not with you—not with anyone—so just get out of the truck. I don't need your shit right now." His words are ice cold, and once again I feel the tears brewing, but I know this definitely isn't the time to release any of my emotion.

Instead, I keep my mouth shut and get out like he asks. The second I slam the door, he mashes the gas and tears off down the street, bypassing his house and going God knows where.

It's quiet inside my house, which is nothing new. Dad always seems to be at work these days. I'm always out and about, and I guess he likes to stay busy. The stillness provides absolutely no distraction, and my thoughts immediately drift to Jared. He needs help, and I'm not sure who the best person to do that is. He has friends, but he always tells me that I'm his best friend—the one person that he confides everything in. The guys on the team are his friends too, but they're not close. There's only one other person that I know who's as close to Jared as I am.

I sigh as I pick up the cordless phone in my living room. Wes answers the Krafts' phone on the third ring.

"Wes, it's London," I tell him. "I'm worried about Jared."

"Join the club," Wes says. "He barely speaks to Mom or me, and whenever we try to talk to him about Dad or what's going on with his scholarship, it turns into a huge shouting match. Mom is worried sick. Have you tried talking to him?"

"Yeah, I tried to, and today didn't go so well with the dean. Jared stormed out—nearly left me behind—and then all but threw me out of the truck when he dropped me off. I'm worried, Wes. It's like he's becoming a different person."

He's quiet for a few moments, but then he says, "I really don't know what to do, London. I want to be there for him, but I'm grieving too—so is Mom, and not once has Jared showed any concern for us. It's like he's got it in his head that he's the only one who lost Dad. He's being a selfish dick. He's making it really hard for me to care about the way he's screwing his life up."

He's frustrated—it's coming through his tone loud and clear, and that worries me. What Wes is saying is true. Jared is being unbelievably selfish right now, but we need to try and look past that to help him if we can. He needs us.

I pick at the bracelet on my wrist as I think carefully about what I need to say next. "You can't give up on him, Wes, even if you think you want to, you just can't. He's your brother, and even though he's not showing it right now, he loves you and Julie so much. I don't know how we can help him if he won't let us, but we have to keep trying. We're all he's got."

A rush of air blows into the phone. "Did he tell you anything about how the meeting went today?"

I twist my lips, reliving earlier today in my head and how much it hurt to see Jared so torn up over the whole situation. "They're yanking his scholarship and he's off the team. Without baseball . . . it's like he's lost and yet another thing's been taken away from him.

God, Wes . . ." I take a deep breath because it's hard to think about just how cold Jared was toward me in his truck. "Jared's freaked out. I've never seen him like this before, and I'm concerned that he might try and do something stupid. I'm really worried about him."

There's a long pause as Wes takes in everything I've said. "Do you have any idea where he might've gone? I can go look for him."

"With how enraged he was earlier, I have no clue. I just hope he didn't go out looking for drugs again, even though he promised me that he will never do that again. Jared developing a drug problem is something we definitely don't need at this point. He's dealing with enough already, and he doesn't need to compound things."

"Will you be at your house?" he asks.

"Yeah, I want to stay here in case he comes back and decides he wants to talk."

"Okay, then I'll go out and look for him."

I bite my bottom lip, glad to have Wes to lean on in this situation. "Thank you, Wes."

"No problem. I'll take Mom's cell phone. Call me if he comes back."

With that, he hangs up and I'm left with nothing to do but wait.

The minutes turn to hours, and the day bleeds into the evening without any sign of Jared. Finally, close to midnight, headlights shine in through the window as Wes's car pulls into my driveway. I glance down the street and frown the minute I don't spot any sign of Jared's truck following behind Wes's car.

Wes shoves his hands into the front pockets of his jeans while his head hangs low, causing his sandy-blond hair to fall into his eyes. Judging by his stance, I don't think he found any trace of his brother.

I pull open the door as he steps up onto my porch, before he even has a chance to knock. "No sign of him?"

He shakes his head. "No. I searched everywhere—even the side of town he got busted on—and didn't find anything. Wherever he is, he doesn't want to be found, that's for sure."

I push the door open wider and motion him inside. "Might as well keep me company as we wait. Hopefully he'll turn up soon."

He steps inside and turns his head to look around my house. "Wow. It's been a while since I've been in here, but things are exactly how I remembered." He points to a picture hanging up next to the door of me from junior high. "I think that's when I first met you— all elbows and knees."

I roll my eyes and laugh as I close the front door. "That was clearly a long time ago."

He smiles and his eyes quickly give me the once-over. "That it was."

Suddenly there's this weird tension between us—something I've never noticed before—and for a split second I worry if having Wes alone with me in the house might give him the wrong impression.

I probably should ask him to leave but decide it's best to blow it off, no sense in making a big deal out of something if I read that entirely wrong. After all, Wes is here to help me find Jared. I need to refocus on that.

I quickly move into being a gracious host. "Would you like something to drink while we wait?"

He shrugs his shoulders. "Sure. Whatever you have is fine."

I head into the kitchen and open the refrigerator. My eyes scan the shelves and I shake my head. I'm going to have to talk with Dad about his eating habits. There's absolutely nothing in this fridge except beer and cheese.

I grab two beers from the carton and make my way back into the living room to hand one of the bottles to Wes. "Hope you like Bud Light. It's all Dad seems to have in his fridge, cold."

He chuckles and takes the beer. "Beer's fine. If I get too hammered, I'll just walk home."

I laugh as I plop down on the couch beside him.

Two beers later, we've nearly finished the carton and I glance up at the clock. Before my eyes zero in on the time, the front door swings open, and in staggers a very drunk Jared. Instantly, I'm on my feet, both relieved and pissed to see him.

"London!" Jared doesn't even look in the direction of the living room where I am. Instead, he shuffles over to the bottom of the stairs and calls for me. "Baby, I'm sorry." It's clear from the slur in his voice that he's completely hammered, and what angers me even more is the fact that he drove home that way.

I'm going to rip him a new ass for being so stupid when he sobers up.

"Jared!" I say, and he jerks his head slowly toward me. "I'm here."

He wobbles and squints one eye like he's trying to focus, and then he points to the beer in my hand. "What are we celebrating? My fucked-up life?"

I set my drink down on the coffee table. "I could ask you the same question."

He flinches and jerks his head back, causing him to wobble and fall into the door frame. "That's exactly why I'm drunk. I'm celebrating how big of a loser I have officially become."

"Jesus, Jared. Did you drive like this?" Wes's agitated voice fills the room, and for the first time Jared notices his brother is even in the same room with us.

Jared's eyes grow dark. "What are you doing here?"

"Waiting for your stupid ass," Wes fires back.

"Waiting for me? You expect me to believe that? I know what you're doing. I see the way you look at her," Jared slurs while his nostrils flare, and I know I have to stop this before it goes any further and he says something that he doesn't mean. These two have done nothing but go at it since they found out about their father. They never used to act like this, and I wish Jared would reel in his anger before something really bad happens.

I step in front of Jared and place my hand on his chest. "Jared, stop. Nothing is going on. You're drunk. Go home and sleep it off."

"I can't leave you here with him. You're all that I've got left." His blue eyes stare down at me. "He's in love with you, London. Don't you see? Now that I'm a complete loser he's going to step in and take you away from me. He's Joe College. He'll have a good job and be the right kind of guy for you."

I shake my head. "You're the right kind of guy for me! Do you think I'm that superficial that I'll just walk out on you now that things are tough? Love doesn't work that way."

He shakes his head, and his words come out just barely above a whisper. "No, I'm not. Not anymore. I'm the kind of worthless piece of shit that your dad probably warned you to stay away from when you were a little girl."

"Stop! Don't talk like that!" I order him. "I think you've lost your mind. Go home and sleep it off."

"No!" he shouts.

I throw my hands on my hips. "Go home!"

"*No!*" he shouts, louder this time. "I'm not leaving you here alone with him."

Wes, sensing my struggle, steps up beside me. "Come on, man. Let's go."

Wes grabs Jared's arm and attempts to turn him back around toward the door, but Jared twists out of his grasp and then shoves his hands into Wes's chest. "Don't fucking touch me or I will end you!"

My eyes widen. "Jared, stop. You're being crazy!"

Jared's head tilts and there's a darkness in his eyes. "Crazy? You think this is me being crazy?"

He walks to the middle of the living room and bends down to pick up the beer I was just drinking off the coffee table. He puts the bottle to his lips and takes a long pull.

"Man, you've had enough." Wes tries again to get through to him.

Jared's shoulders tense and then he stares down at the drink in his hand. Without warning, Jared turns on his heel and wings the bottle in Wes's direction. Wes ducks just in time for the bottle to smash against the wall, shattering the glass and knocking the picture of me off the wall. Liquid drips down, and as I stare at it, my sympathy for what Jared's going through disappears.

He's crossing a line. I don't even know this guy. The Jared I know would never disrespect my house like this, drunk or not.

My heart thunders inside my chest and I march over and smack Jared right across the face. "Get out!"

"No!" he challenges me again. "Tell him to leave first."

I shove on his chest as hard as I can, but he's a complete wall of muscle and I can't budge him.

Once again, Wes tries to intervene, which instantly throws Jared into a deeper rage. The moment Wes grabs my arms to pull me back, Jared reaches over my shoulder and shoves Wes. "I told you, don't fucking touch her."

"Do you even hear yourself right now?" Wes asks. "You're losing your shit. Go home before you do something that you regret."

Jared narrows his eyes. "Who the fuck do you think you are? You are not my father. He's dead, remember?"

Things from this point on happen so quickly, it all seems like a blur. The second the words leave Jared's lips, Wes shoves me to the side and then blasts Jared in the face with a hard right hook. Jared falls back from the impact and slams through the glass coffee table, throwing little shards in every direction.

I cover my face with my hands, unsure of how hurt he is as he lies there for a split second. Jared's not down long. He pops back up and barrels into Wes, wrapping his arms around him and tackling him so hard that I hear the crunch of bone on bone on impact. Both men fall to the floor, and all I see are fists flying as they roll around.

This is a situation that I never in my wildest dreams imagined. They've never fought before . . . not like this anyway. Sure, they've had arguments, but this is . . . unbelievable. When Jared comes to his senses, he's going to regret this. I have to stop it before one of them gets hurt.

I bend down and wrap my arms around Jared's neck, doing my best to stop him from beating the shit out of his brother. It's at that very moment he cocks his arm back to land another blow to Wes's face, and his elbow catches me right in the temple and the world goes black.

*NOW*
**JARED**

**B**ells chime as I push the door to Mom's shop open. I stare down at the handle and smile. They're the bells I used in a Christmas pageant for our church when I was in the third grade. I hated those damn bells, but it had made Mom so happy that I'd volunteered to be in the pageant that I couldn't take it back and beg her to not make me do it even after they assigned me to play those stupid bells.

"Be right with you," Mom calls from the back room where she does all her prep work.

I open my mouth to tell her it's me but decide against it because I figure she's wrapping up something important.

I take my time walking around the shop. Everywhere I look there's some flower arrangement or some amazing display of baked goods—each one more artistic and beautiful than the last. Her skills have really evolved. She took on arranging flowers to go along with the candies to bring in more money. Selling the candies alone wasn't enough to pay all the bills without Dad's income.

On the wall behind the counter, there's an array of photos of different events. Most look like weddings, and from what I can tell, Mom has provided flowers and desserts for several fancy events.

One wedding photo catches my attention—what I think is the groom in particular. The picture isn't centered on him, but he's standing next to a large floral arch as he stares down the aisle at what I assume is his bride. The guy in the picture—he looks a lot like Wes, just a little older. Surely if my older brother had gotten married, Mom would have figured out a way to slip that into one of our conversations over the past five years.

I lean in a little closer to inspect the photo, and I'm convinced it's him. All the same features are present: the sandy-blond hair, same brown eyes. Hell, the man had even folded his hands in front of himself in the way Wes does.

"Jared?" Mom's voice from the doorway leading to the back catches me off guard.

I straighten up, my eyes meeting her gaze. She looks almost the same as I remember her, only there are a few more prominent lines around the corners of her eyes and mouth. Her dark hair is pulled back into a low ponytail, and her blue eyes glisten with unshed tears at the sight of me standing here.

I give her a small smile. "Hi, Mom."

Unable to hide her excitement, she squeals as she makes her way around the counter and wraps me in one of the tightest hugs known to mankind. She buries her face in my neck and holds me tight against her petite frame. "My boy is home. Thank you, Lord. Thank you."

She continues to chant over and over like her longtime prayers have finally been answered, and it chokes me up a bit to know that she's been waiting for this day so badly. It makes me feel like a completely shitty asshole for not coming to see her sooner. I shouldn't have waited so long. I won't do that again, even if it is difficult for me to come back.

I'm a selfish prick, but I swear from this point on I will not let my mother down like this again. She's too good of a person, and she doesn't deserve the callous way I've treated her.

I wrap my arms around her. "It's so good to see you, Mom. I've missed you."

"Jared." She says my name in a choked-up voice, and I know she's crying even though I can't see her face. "I've missed you so much—more than you can ever possibly know."

We stay like that for a long time, neither of us wanting to let go, and I know that no matter how much I miss Dad or how hard being here without him is, I won't be able to stay away this long ever again.

I spend the rest of the afternoon with Mom in the shop. Neither of us talk about the past. It's like she understands that I need a clean slate in order to feel comfortable here. However, I do learn a lot about the shop.

It's been tough for Mom to keep help around because she can't afford to pay them much more than minimum wage.

I box up a few of the candies after Mom prepares the boxes. She smiles at me, and I can tell she's enjoying me working alongside her. "Do you need to call someone to pick up all these orders for delivery?"

Mom sighs. "Typically, yes. I have an older gentleman who does that, but he called me earlier and said he was really sick today, so after we're done, I'll deliver them."

I shake my head. "That's silly. I'm right here, put me to work. I'll make all the deliveries for you."

"People might recognize you," she says. "I don't want that trouble for you."

I shake my head. "I rarely get noticed unless I'm at an event where people are specifically looking for me. Ace is the face of the band, so he's the one all the media bugs."

Mom nods. She knows what's going on with Wicked White and how Ace was given my spot as the front man of the band, so it's nice that I can talk with her openly about things.

She smiles and her shoulders relax. "Oh, honey. That will help me so much, but please, don't feel like you have to."

"It's no problem. Really. It'll be a good excuse for me to drive around the city and see what's new since I left."

Mom gets right to work lining up all the deliveries and helping me put the cards inside envelopes with addresses on them. I pull the shop's delivery van around to the back door and begin loading things up with Mom's help.

We're nearly done when the phone rings. Mom motions to the counter where a few prepared arrangements sit next to some of the candies. "That should be the last of it. If you want to get going while I take this call, you can."

I nod. "I'll come back as soon as I'm done, and I'll take you out to dinner."

"Okay, honey." She touches the side of my face and smiles before she rushes to answer the phone.

I turn and grab the rest of the flowers and load them into my arms. One bundle of yellow roses sits off to the side. I grab those too, figuring Mom just missed them, double-check that there's an address on the card, and then head out to the van to start getting all these flowers to the lucky recipients.

## *THEN*
## JARED

Even in my drunken state, I know I've just royally fucked up the moment London releases me and falls to the floor. There's a sting in my elbow from where I made contact with something behind me, and it's not hard to figure out that I just plowed into London in my fit of rage.

Wes shoves me off of him, and there's sheer panic in his voice. "What the fuck did you do?"

He scrambles to his knees and crawls over to London, who lies motionless on the living room floor. Wes scoops his arm under her shoulders and lifts her head up off the floor. This doesn't awaken her at all. Her head drops back as Wes says her name over and over.

Oh, shit, what have I done?

I squat down beside her and place my hand on her chest to feel it rise and fall. When I know she's breathing, I wrap my arms around her, hug her to my body, and kiss her face. "Oh, God. London, I'm so sorry." I bury my face into her dark hair and sob. "Please wake up. I'm so sorry. So sorry."

I say it over and over again like a chant before I squeeze my eyes shut and scold myself for being drunk. Everything feels like it's in slow motion, and I'm not in my right mind to know how to help her.

Wes jerks his gaze toward me. "Don't just sit there! Get off your ass and call nine-one-one!"

His brash tone grabs my attention as I sit there in horror, realizing that I've just hurt the one person that I love most in this world. If things keep going like this . . . if I keep fucking up . . . I am going to ruin her life, and that's the last thing I ever want to do.

"Jared!" Wes's voice cuts through my groggy thought process. "Make the Goddamn call!"

I shake my head as if to try and shake some sense into it as I push myself up off the floor. I grab the phone and quickly dial the number to get help.

"Nine-one-one, what's your emergency?" the female operator calmly asks from the other end of the line.

"Um, we need an ambulance. My girlfriend . . . she's hurt," I say.

"Is she injured?" the woman asks.

I stare down at London's limp body in Wes's arms. "Yes. She got hit in the head."

"Is she breathing?"

"Yes."

"Okay, sir, I'm sending someone right now. I'll need you to tell me where she was struck . . ."

The operator goes on and on, but I'm so focused on London that I don't process everything the woman on the phone is telling me. I need her to wake up—I need to know that she's okay. I won't be able to live with myself if I hurt her.

"Sir . . . sir?"

God knows my brother, who is clearly in love with London, will never forgive me for this. He's going to hate me forever . . . and

Mom . . . God, I don't want to see the look on her face when she finds out that I've disappointed her again. It was so hard to see it the day she picked me up from jail. I never want to see that in her eyes again.

I don't think I can take it.

London stirs on the floor, and I can tell she's starting to come to. I can't face her—not after what I did—and my face is probably the last thing she wants to see right now.

I drop the phone down by Wes's side, and he stares up at me with an expression that can only be labeled as confused. "What the hell?"

"I can't . . ." That's all I can manage to say before I turn on my heel and walk out the door.

I'm so out of control right now. I'm putting the woman I love in danger, and I won't allow anything to hurt her ever again—including me.

"Jared!" Wes screams from the other side of the door, but I keep going without looking back.

Unable to go back home, I hop in my truck and drive around the corner and park to sleep off all the liquor I drank. I'm not sure how long I was out, but a pounding on my window jerks me out of a deep sleep. Beams of sunlight shine in my face, so I have to squint as I roll down the window. When my vision comes into focus, the girl I met a few days ago with jet-black hair and the pink stripe stands there with her hands on her hips. Her all-black appearance screams rocker, and the matching skull-and-crossbones earrings make her outfit complete.

"You again," she says as she snaps her gum. "Does this mean you want to join the band?"

Completely confused, I raise one eyebrow. "Huh?"

She motions to the small blue house behind her. "This is the address on the card I gave you for the band, remember?"

Mentally I flip back through when I met her, and a name comes to mind. "Lick Me and Split?"

She nods with a grin on her face. "Catchy, right? So are you in? We're leaving to head out on tour." She points in front of my truck to where a bunch of other girls dressed in the same fashion as her take turns loading different instruments into the back. "We got a break playing a few shows in Nashville, opening up for some newly signed band for Mopar Records. They're called Black Falcon, and they're supposedly some group of badass hard rock guys. From everything I read about them online, looks like the women love them, which will be good for us. Plus they're signed to a record label, so we're sure to get some exposure—might even get us signed."

I tilt my head. "How does a legion of fangirls work out in your favor?"

She smiles. "More hot groupie chicks with big boobs for us to pick from." My mouth falls open, causing her to cackle. "So what do you say, Joe College? You in or out?"

I debate her offer. It's almost like it's been sent to me at the right time, because I desperately need to get out of this town. The truth is, though, I don't know this chick from Adam. She could be completely insane—well . . . that's probably true. I mean, look how easily she approached me on campus and then invited me out on the road with her even though I'm a complete stranger. Who does shit like that? Crazy girls, that's who.

She is easy to talk to, and it seems like she's batting for the other team, so I don't think she's inviting me along as a come-on. Maybe I should go. Maybe this will be a good way for me to stop inflicting pain on the ones I love and refocus while I'm away—get my head right again.

A tall blond with cropped hair slams the doors to the van shut and turns in our direction. "All loaded up. Let's roll!"

The rocker chick turns back to me and raises her eyebrows, waiting for my answer. "Time's up."

"I'm in," I tell her without any hesitation.

She grins. "Awesome. Follow us, and try to keep up."

Without another word, she turns and heads toward the van. It hits me then that I don't even know the first thing about this girl, and if we're going to be in a band together, a little introduction would be good.

I stick my head out the window. "What's your name?"

She turns but keeps walking backward in her Doc Martens. "Suzie Q! Yours?"

"Jared," I tell her.

She gives me a thumbs-up as she skips off to the van, and I fire up my truck, ready to head out and start a new life—one that if I screw up, the only person it hurts is me.

## THEN
## LONDON

Follow the light with your eyes," the doctor in the white lab coat instructs as I sit on the edge of the gurney in the emergency room.

He moves the penlight up and down and side to side before bringing it in to almost touch my nose, causing my eyes to strain.

"Good," he says as he steps back and then shoves the penlight into the pocket of his jacket. "It doesn't seem like there are any long-term effects. That must have been some fall. It's crazy that you hit your head just at the right angle to knock yourself out. Try to be more careful and limit your alcohol intake." He writes something down on a little notepad and then tears off the sheet of paper before handing it to me. "Here's a prescription for ibuprofen, eight hundred milligrams, for pain. You can take one every four to six hours."

I take the paper. "Thanks, but like I said, I feel completely fine."

"I want you to follow up with your family doctor in the next two to three days, and if you notice any odd changes in vision or motor skill, report back here immediately so we can do that CT scan that you refused." The doctor pats me on the shoulder. "Take care, London."

The second he leaves the room, I hop off the table. Wes puts his arms around me to make sure I'm steady. "You good?"

I nod. "I'm completely fine."

Wes frowns. "Why did you lie to the paramedics about what happened to you?"

I shrug as we make our way down the hall of the hospital toward the exit. "It was an accident, Wes. I don't need anyone questioning Jared about it. He's gone through enough."

He shakes his head. "Always protecting him. At some point, London, Jared is going to have to take responsibility for his actions. Both you and Mom coddle him far too much, and it's not helping. It doesn't force him to face things like a grown adult. It's like he throws little tantrums and gets out of things, but when the law steps in—there's no getting out of that."

I've never heard Wes talk about his brother like this before. "You act like Jared has always been this way. He's not a spoiled brat, Wes. All this—the things he's going through—he's never been like this before."

Wes pushes open the thick glass door to the outside and holds it for me. "He's always been selfish, London. You just didn't allow yourself to see it before because you were blinded by your love for him. You always gave in and did exactly what he wanted you to do."

We make our way to Wes's car, and I furrow my brow. "Name one situation where I sacrificed something I wanted to make Jared happy."

"That's easy. College."

"College?" I repeat. "What about it?"

Wes opens the passenger door to his four-door black sedan. "Did you really want to go to the University of Tennessee?" I open my mouth to protest immediately, but the look on Wes's face tells me to not bullshit him. "Be honest."

"Not at first, no, I guess, but once Jared and I talked about it, it made sense for us to both go there, seeing as I didn't have a car. Besides, I wanted to stay close to him."

"Exactly my point," Wes chimes in. "You at first wanted to go to art school, not to a traditional four-year school, but Jared made you change your mind to bend to what he wanted. You gave up your dream of being an artist to study early childhood education just to go to the same school he did."

He's got me there. "That may be true, but I love working with the kids when I go out and do my actual student teaching. They are simply precious. And, believe it or not, I do get to be creative doing that job. I love evoking the kids' love of art. The expressions on their faces—how proud they are—when they create something are inspiring. Besides, just because I didn't officially study art doesn't mean that I'm not an artist. I can still do it on the side."

I take a seat in the car, and Wes leans against the open door. "You are an amazing person, London, and I don't think Jared fully appreciates what he has. Please think about setting your foot down. I know he's had a hard time lately, but I lost my dad too, and Mom her husband and best friend. You don't see us acting insane. It makes me worry—this new side of him. The way his anger can come out so quickly when things don't go his way. I worry about the kind of life you'll have with him. Especially now that everything he's ever known has changed."

Wes has always been the sweet Kraft brother—the polite one everyone thought highly of when we were in high school. His younger brother overshadowed him a lot because he was the baseball star. I guess I myself am guilty of never noticing how sweet he is. His concern for me now is unbelievably heartwarming and opens my eyes to the point Jared was trying to make in his drunken state: maybe Wes is in love with me.

I stare up into his caring eyes, which remind me so much of Jared's, and nod. "I promise that I'll speak with him—try to get him to refocus his anger somewhere and convince him to talk with someone. I think that he needs some professional help dealing with everything that's happened in this short amount of time."

He seems satisfied with that answer. "Good. I love you both and I want to see you both happy, even if that means the two of you are no longer together."

My heart crumbles at the mere thought of Jared and me not being together. I've loved him since I was in junior high, and being without him isn't something that even registers on my radar. It's not a possibility that I will think about entertaining, even in bad times like this when he runs out on me.

Wes offers to take me to his house because he wants to be around to watch over me and make sure that I'm okay. Only when he pulls up in the drive and discovers that my dad is home does he let me go in alone.

He comes around and opens my door, sticking close to my side as we walk up the sidewalk and get to my front door. When I open the door and push myself inside, I freeze when my eyes land on the disaster in my living room. There's glass everywhere—on the wall where Jared threw the bottle, in the middle of the floor where Jared crashed through the glass coffee table.

Dad comes in from the kitchen with a broom and dustpan in hand. "Do you know what in the hell happened in here? I walked through the door and saw this mess, and my very first thought was that we'd been robbed, but after I checked the house and saw nothing was missing, I came to the conclusion that there must've been a raging party in here."

"Mr. Uphill, sir, it's partly my fault, and I will clean every bit of this mess up," Wes says.

Dad scratches the top of his head. "You, Wes? I don't see this kind of behavior coming from you. It looks like there was some sort of fight in here."

Wes grimaces. "That's because there was. Jared and I had a misunderstanding."

Dad's eyes flick over in my direction, and I can tell he knows there's more to the story than that. "A misunderstanding, huh? Care to tell me what had the two of you so worked up that you destroyed my house?"

Wes licks his lips. "Jared had the wrong idea about me being here alone with London. He was drunk and things got completely out of hand."

Dad rubs his fingers over the scruff on his lower chin. "I see. So where is Jared now?"

I shrug. "I don't know. He took off after the fight, and I haven't heard from him since."

I purposefully leave off the little detail of me getting hit and going to the hospital for now, even though I know I won't be able to keep that part a secret forever, considering the bills from the hospital will come soon enough.

"He seems to be doing that a lot lately," Dad says. "He's lost a lot of my respect for the way he's treating his mother after all she's been through. The boy doesn't seem to have his head on straight. He's got to pull it together. Getting caught with the drugs . . . it's just something I can't overlook as a man of the law, and it's making me question his integrity and whether or not I want him with my daughter."

"Dad, that's not up to you," I fire back. "I love Jared, and I know he's going to pull through this. We just can't give up on him."

"London." Dad says my name with a sigh. "Sometimes when tragedy strikes, a person has a hard time coming back from it, and if they do, they're never the same. I know Jared was close with his dad, but if Henry could see the way he's screwing up, he wouldn't be happy either. He would tell the kid to get his shit together, and when I see him again, that's exactly what I'm going to say."

I want to beg him not to say that to Jared—to trust in the fact that Jared will redeem himself—but I know Dad's in the right. Jared does need to get his shit together before he ruins everything and every bit of trust that I have in him.

Dad takes the broom and shoves the glass into a pile and doesn't ask any more questions about the situation. That's the one thing about Dad, he doesn't pry too much, but when there is an issue he always tries to resolve it quickly.

I guess that's where I get the fixer in me—from Dad.

The night goes on much the same, none of us talking about what happened here. We just work to get it all cleaned up, and after we're done and have said good-bye to Wes, I head off to bed, completely exhausted from the events of the day.

As soon as my head hits the pillow, I find that I am unable to force my eyes shut. My brain is still wide awake as I ponder where Jared could be and what I'll say the next time I see him.

The next day comes and goes without a word from Jared. I consider going out and combing the streets looking for him again, but I've learned from the last two times I went out to find him that it doesn't seem to do any good.

After two days, I begin to seriously worry. No one has seen him—I mean, absolutely no one. It's like he's fallen off the face of the earth.

On the third day, I can no longer take just sitting back and wondering what's happened to him. Since Dad is a cop, I plead with him to allow me to file a missing persons report. It takes some convincing, but after I explain that I've searched everywhere and I can find no sign of him, he agrees that it might be a good idea to let everyone know he's missing. I mean, he could be hurt somewhere, and Dad knows that being gone for this long isn't in Jared's character.

A month goes by, and we've had no luck in finding Jared. Everyone is beginning to expect the worst since there's been no sign of him.

Summer break eventually rolls around, and with still no word from Jared, I volunteer to clear his dorm room out. My hope is beginning to fade, and it's becoming clear to me that wherever he is, he doesn't want to be found. The chances of him returning to school next semester are slight.

"Are you sure you don't need my help?" Julie asks as she pulls into the parking lot just outside the dorm. "Don't mind spending a couple hours packing up Jared's room."

I shake my head. "I can do it. Besides, you have a lot going on at the shop—just swing by after you're done and I'll load up your car with boxes."

She sighs. "Okay, but call me if you change your mind and need my help. I really don't mind. He is my son, after all—no matter where he is."

I reach over and take her hand. "He's going to turn up, Julie."

Tears glisten in her eyes. "I hope so. I don't think I can take the loss of someone else so close to me. My heart won't survive it a second time."

I can't believe that Jared would do this to his mother, or to me. We both love him, and it's like our love for him wasn't good enough to keep him here. It makes me wonder how much he really cared for me in the first place. If I were in his position, no matter how hopeless things seemed, I would fight hard to keep my relationship with Jared alive because I love him with every inch of my heart. It hurts that he doesn't feel the same, and if I could, I would kick my own ass for still loving him so much.

I sigh as I look at Julie's face and watch the tears stream down her cheeks. No matter how angry I am at Jared, I still love him—Julie and I both do—and we need to find him to make sure he knows that we haven't given up on him.

It's then I decide I need to step it up and figure out a way to find Jared, not just for my sake, but for Julie's too. It breaks my heart even more to see her so sad. I have to know that he's all right.

*THEN*
**JARED**

**S**uzie Q wasn't kidding when she said the women go mad over these Black Falcon guys. Every show we open for these guys in Nashville, the place is packed with women. Suzie Q and the rest of the chicks in the band have been having a field day trying to turn all these straight women out.

They've got some serious game, and I think they're well on their way to becoming notorious ladies' women . . . or however you want to label them.

Suzie Q screams into the microphone, "We're Lick Me and Split. Thanks for coming out to see us! Make sure you stop over at our merchandise booth and say hello! Good night!"

I play the last few riffs in time with the drumbeats and then head off stage. We're still very, very rough as a cohesive band, but I think we've come together quite well in the past few weeks. I've even gotten better with singing on stage with the band in front of crowds. It's a big change from singing solo and playing acoustically, but I can see this as being a new dream for me—making it in the music business since baseball is further out of reach for a future career. Besides, playing ball doesn't feel the same without Dad around.

Standing just to the side of the stage is a woman in a skintight red leather skirt with an equally tight red blouse to match. She must really be into red, considering her hair is also the same color. When I pass by, the woman smiles at me the moment we make eye contact. While I can honestly say she's not my type, she's attractive for a woman who has at least fifteen years on me.

"That was an amazing set. The girls really seem to be into you," the redhead says to me.

When she points to the crowd behind her, I notice a lot of the women are still looking in my direction. I turn my attention back to the woman in red. "Thanks. I'm glad you enjoyed it."

At that point I imagine we're done with the conversation because I don't instantly feed into the woman's compliments and hit on her, but instead she reaches into her purse and whips out a business card. "My name is Jane Ann Rogers, and I work for Mopar Records. I'm scouting for new talent for a special project that the label is working on. We're putting together a band, and I'm looking for a front man—a guy with that 'it' thing that will pull people in. I think you might be the man I'm looking for."

I raise my eyebrows and then stare down at the very official-looking business card. This is the record label that represents Black Falcon. Mopar Records has been making big waves signing new bands as of late, so her proposition definitely piques my interest. "You want me?"

"Yes. I think you're exactly right. Come down to the office in Nashville Monday morning at nine sharp, and we'll talk more."

I flick the card between my fingers and smile. "Okay. Thank you. I'll be there."

Just as quickly as she appeared, she disappears into the crowd, leaving me elated.

"Who was that?" Suzie Q asks. "She was hot in that cougar kind of way."

My first instinct is to bust out with the good news, but then I think better of it when I remember that the offer Jane Ann Rogers extended a moment ago was only to me and not to the rest of the band. It would make me a humongous asshole to rub in the fact that I just got propositioned to come talk business with a record company and the rest of the band didn't.

I stuff the card into my back pocket and shrug. "She wanted to share a bed with me for the night."

Suzie Q's eyes light up, and she punches my shoulder. "Sweet! Are you going to tap that? I want video if you do. I bet she's all kinds of freaky."

I roll my eyes and laugh. "Hate to burst your bubble, but I turned her down."

She sighs, clearly unhappy with my answer. "You turn down every single chick that comes in here. Why is that? You still got a thing going with that girl I spotted you with on campus when I first met you?"

The mere mention of London causes my back to stiffen. That's been the hardest part about starting over—trying to pretend that every beat of my heart isn't dedicated to loving London—but I can't be with her when I can't be myself. *I* don't even know who I am anymore. How can I ask her to continue to love a man that neither of us really knows? Dad dying shook the foundation of my life, and London was integral to that part of me. I need to start over, figure out who I am, before I can possibly even begin to fathom moving on. It wouldn't have been fair of me to ask London to wait around until I figured my shit out. I still feel so lost inside. If only Dad were here so I could call him up and get some advice about the situation.

The last thought trips me up. If Dad were still here, I doubt I would be in this situation in the first place. Losing him is what started me on this downward spiral and pushed me into that dark place where I lost my head and acted crazy for a while.

I feel like I'm just now beginning to think straight, and being out of the situation and away from everyone who reminds me of how things used to be has allowed me to get my head a little clearer. I've still got a long way to go.

I shake my head. "No. There's absolutely nothing going on between her and me."

She raises one eyebrow. "Well, then, I think it's time to live it up, starting with that blond with amazing tits who's been eye-fucking you since we stepped on stage."

"Where?" I ask as I turn and scan the crowd.

Suzie Q raises her hand and points her index finger to the other side of the room, where a blond woman sits at the bar in a too-short skirt and her breasts practically hanging out of her top. The moment we make eye contact she licks her lips, and there's no doubt what she wants from me.

I swallow hard. If I go through with this—if I sleep with this woman—she will be the only person I've ever been with other than London. But I've got to force London out of my mind. I can't allow myself to think about her anymore. Come hell or high water, I must embrace this new life, regardless of if I'm still irrevocably in love with London. It's the only way I can move on.

Almost as if on autopilot, I head in the blond's direction. She grins, revealing nearly perfect white teeth, clearly happy that I'm heading her way.

"Get it," Suzie Q shouts in encouragement as I walk away.

I take a seat next to her at the bar, and at first I feel uneasy about flirting with her—it feels wrong—but I push through the odd feeling and give her my most charming smile after I order a drink. "Did you enjoy the show?"

Her eyes light up. "Oh, yeah. I particularly liked watching you. The way you move when you play, topped off by the way you sing— it's hypnotic."

The compliment causes me to genuinely smile as the bartender sets my beer in front of me. "Thanks. That's always a great thing to hear."

"I mean that. You're total eye candy, and I wouldn't mind taking a bite of you," she says as she leans in and places a hand on my biceps. "Just like I thought—you're totally buff. Your muscles are huge. Does the rest of you match?"

I choke on my beer and quickly set it down on the bar. "Wow. You don't fuck around, do you?"

"I'm a cut-right-to-the-chase kind of girl. When I see something that I want, I just go for it, full throttle."

I quirk one brow. "And what is it exactly that you want from me?"

Her grin turns devilish. "I think you already know the answer to that question. The question is, are you willing to give it to me?"

I take another swallow of my beer and then set it back down. I've had my fair share of women throwing themselves at me when I was in college playing ball, but nothing compares to the women in the rock scene. They all seem so willing.

This is like every man's fantasy—approach the hot blond and have her be ready and willing in that very moment. This chick has made it very clear to me she wants to fuck. The question is: Do I want to go through with it?

I nod toward her empty glass. "Buy you a drink?"

She licks her lips seductively. "You can give me whatever you want, sugar."

About an hour and five beers later, I find the blond sitting on my lap. Her arm is thrown around my neck, and every now and then she leans in and presses her lips to some of my exposed flesh. Her fingers idly trail up and down my chest. The more we sit here in this bar together, the more both of us are getting turned on and the easier the idea of fucking this woman becomes.

Soon, I think the woman's patience with me expires, because she hops off my lap and grabs my hand. "Come with me."

I follow her in my drunken haze and allow her to pull me all the way outside. When the cool night air washes over me, I find myself being pushed back against the brick wall and attacked with lips.

Completely lost in the moment, I allow my hands to slide down her back to find her ass and squeeze each of her cheeks. This only excites her more, and she hitches one leg on my hip and grinds her pussy against my crotch.

She giggles while her lips remain pressed to mine. "Your cock is huge. This is going to be so much fun."

There's no denying that I have a raging hard-on right now, and it's throbbing with anticipation to find its way inside this woman. "We can't do this here."

"No problem," she says and pulls back, grabbing my hand again. "I've got a car in the parking lot." She leads me out a ways from the building to a shiny black Mustang. She unlocks the door and then shoves forward the driver's seat. "There's more room in the back."

I lick my lips and hesitate for a fraction of a second. Once I go in there, I know there's no going back—no way to turn back from sleeping with another woman. London will hate me forever if she finds out.

London Uphill is the complete opposite of my new companion— hell, I don't even know this woman's name yet. London is sweet and caring, where this woman is definitely not sweet, and if I had to guess, she's running from something too—something she doesn't want to remember. This woman is dragging a complete stranger to her car, so I don't feel guilty that I'm using her for a distraction, because it's obvious that she's just using me too.

I relax my shoulders and head into the backseat.

## *THEN*
## **LONDON**

I stare down at the address and study the numbers on the outside of the building. "Are you sure this is the place?" My eyes trail over the dilapidated wood siding and wonder how the bar remains open based on its outside appearance.

"Yes," Wes says. "Look at all the cars in the parking lot. This was where the private investigator tracked him to. He said the band that Jared has been traveling with is playing here tonight."

It's hard to imagine Jared in here—not saying that he hasn't done some shady shit lately. When I think of Jared, I picture him happy, smiling, and on the baseball field—the one place he loved. This is definitely a new lifestyle choice for him.

I take a deep breath and then release it through pursed lips. "We might as well go in there and see if we can find him. Remember to keep your cool. Our goal is to convince him to come back with us. Being hostile and losing your temper, no matter how much he's made Julie cry—"

"And you," Wes adds in. "Let's not forget that."

"And me," I say in agreement. "We have to try to bring him out of whatever dark place he's in."

"I swear. I'll be good. I won't even say a word to him. I'll let you do all the talking. How's that?"

"That might be best." I grab the handle on the passenger door and push it open. "Come on."

We had to park in the very back of the lot in the grass. Seems like this is the place to be tonight, which in an odd way makes me proud. I always knew that Jared had a massive amount of talent, so it's good that other people in the world are getting to experience just how musically gifted he is.

We're nearly to the building when a door on a black Mustang flings open as we walk by, nearly hitting Wes.

"Whoa," Wes says as he quickly jumps out of the way.

"Oh, sorry, man," a voice from inside the car calls out, and it instantly halts me in my tracks. "Didn't see you there."

A very feminine giggle follows the voice. "You almost hit that guy."

"I know." The man laughs, and my blood runs cold.

My gaze flicks up to Wes, and his mouth drops open in shock. I turn to peek inside the car, but Wes grabs my shoulder and pulls me back. "Don't. You don't want to do that."

I know he thinks he's protecting me from what is inside that car, but I have to see it with my own two eyes. "I have to."

"London—" Wes pleads as I twist out of his grasp and then bend down to look inside.

I stand there completely frozen, staring at the sight before me. Jared is sitting in the backseat with a blond woman straddling his lap. She has only a bra on, while the skirt she's wearing is shoved up around her waist. She has no underwear on, and Jared's pants are shoved down around his ankles.

I stand there watching, unable to look away even though the

sight of this is absolutely tearing me up inside. Neither Jared nor the woman have any idea that I'm there—both completely oblivious that my heart is being smashed in my chest right now—because they are both completely hammered, which still doesn't excuse Jared's behavior.

Jared laughs, trying to help her put her top back on.

Seeing this sight before me drives home the fact that I need to move on, because obviously he has.

"You've got your head in the arm hole." He yanks the shirt back off and then slides it back onto the woman.

She pulls it down, covering most of her torso. "You're so smart." She leans in and kisses him. "And sexy." Another kiss. "And a good fuck."

"That's enough." Wes's voice wafts through my clouded brain just before he pulls me away from the car, but not fast enough to miss Jared's eyes snapping in my direction. "Don't do this to yourself, London. He's not worth it. He's a prick."

Tears burn my eyes, and for the first time in my life, I no longer give a shit about Jared Kraft. I'm so angry that I'm sure in this moment I can walk away and never think about him ever again.

Jared's voice ordering the woman off of him echoes around the empty parking lot, and I begin to shake. This is not the man who loved me. This is not the man who asked me to marry him and then gave me a ring—this is not the man I love.

Wes attempts to pull me back toward his car, but anger rages through me. The thought of storming over there and grabbing hand-fuls of Jared's now-shaggy hair and dragging him out of the car crosses my mind, but I know that's the absolute wrong thing to do. I need him to hurt—to feel the pain I'm feeling right now.

I stare down at the ring on my finger and hate that its sparkle is now gone.

The woman gets out of the car first, followed by Jared, who stares in our direction with a furrowed brow. "What in the hell are the two of you doing here?"

I open my mouth to fire back at him, but Wes turns me around and points me in the direction of his car again. "He's drunk, London. Don't get him started. We've seen how things go when he's drunk and angry, and I won't allow him to hurt you again—accident or not."

We march toward Wes's car, and all the while I fight the urge to run back and smack the shit out of Jared's face.

"Don't ever come near me again," Jared yells across the parking lot, and I completely snap.

I twist out of Wes's grip and run back toward Jared, yanking the ring off my finger in the process. "You are a selfish son of a bitch. We thought you were dead! You walk out on all of us with no note—no nothing—after what this family has been through. Your mother hired a private investigator to find out if you were still even alive."

"You are not my family," he growls.

His cold tone causes me to flinch.

*"Who are you?"* I shake my head, completely floored. "I stood by you—told everyone that you were just going through something and that you would get your shit together and grow out of"—I motion up and down his body—"this. But now I can see that I was wrong. You truly don't care about anyone but yourself. Here!" I throw the ring into his chest, and he catches it easily with one hand. "Maybe you can give this to her and tell her a bunch of lies, because I'm done. I never want to ever see you again."

A grimace is the only reaction I get from Jared before he becomes a complete void. A normal person would show some kind of emotion in this situation, but he just stands there without any expression, like I'm annoying him and he can't wait to be rid of me.

I turn on my heel, refusing to allow myself to cry in front of him. I will not break down in front of a man who obviously doesn't care about my feelings.

A small part of me expects Jared to come to his senses and realize how much he's hurt me and his family and chase after me and beg forgiveness for everything that he's put us through. But he doesn't. He allows both me and Wes to walk away, get into the car, and drive off, without any protest whatsoever.

I am so fucking done.

## NOW
## LONDON

I love each and every child in my class, but I am truly grateful when Saturdays roll around for a little bit of a break.

I plop down on the sofa and grab the remote. On the weekends, I never go anywhere or do anything, so the DVR box and I have become besties. I glance up at the clock and notice it's nearly five in the evening, and yet I'm still in my frog-print pajama bottoms and matching tank top, while my hair remains in the same messy bun I put it in this morning. No one will be seeing me, so it's not like it matters.

I stir the chocolate syrup into my chocolate ice cream before I shove a big spoonful into my mouth. This is totally unhealthy, I know, but things have just been so shitty lately, I might as well enjoy something.

Who needs to be a size zero anyhow?

I fast-forward through another set of commercials during my *Vampire Diaries* binge-watch session as I anxiously wait to discover if Elena will finally make a move on Damon, the hot bad-boy brother.

The second I hit "Play," my doorbell rings, causing me to groan as I pause the show.

I set my bowl down on the coffee table, then shove myself up from the couch. The only person who could be at my door is Bud, Julie's sweet delivery man. Poor old guy gets stuck bringing me yellow roses and candy every day, thanks to Wes's over-the-top attempt to keep himself fresh in my mind.

I grab the hair inside the elastic band to tighten it down more so that I appear somewhat presentable. "Coming!"

I grab a couple bucks out of my wallet for a tip, then scuffle over to the door in my bare feet. I twist the knob and push open the door, and the person who's on the other side stops me and steals my breath.

My mouth drops open, and I can't do anything but stare. It's like seeing a ghost—something you never in your life ever expected to see—and I just can't look away. I resist the urge to reach down and pinch myself to make sure this moment is real.

Is this his idea of some twisted joke? I mean, there's no way in hell that Jared Kraft is standing in my doorway with a dozen yellow roses after five years without a single word.

Shit like that only happens in movies, and my life for damn sure isn't some glamorous fairy tale.

I stand there, staring like an idiot, while my brain tries to work out exactly what's going on here. I furrow my brow. This has to be a fucking dream. No way this man has the nerve to just show up here like this—not after all this time.

I step back and take a long moment to study his face. He looks exactly the same as the last time I saw him, only his hair is longer—more shaggy and unkempt—the style I've seen him wear whenever I see pictures of him with his band, Wicked White. To prove to myself that this really is a dream, I reach down and bunch some skin up on my arm and then pinch with all my might.

"Ouch!" I yelp as I inspect the flesh my nails dug into.

My breath catches the moment I realize that the man who used to be my everything—the man who took off five years ago, leaving me and his family behind without so much as a good-bye or piss off—is standing on my porch.

When my eyes meet his, so many questions rage through my mind, but before I can open my mouth to ask a single one, anger begins to boil over inside me. How dare he just come waltzing into my life after all this time?

My body reacts of its own accord and my hand darts out to snatch the flowers out of his hand. His eyes grow wider when I slam them down onto my porch and then smack his face as hard as I can.

My hand instantly stings, but one hit just wasn't enough to make him feel all the pain I felt these past years.

I draw back to hit him again, but he grabs my wrist, yanking my body flush against his, which only further pisses me off. "Let go of me!"

"No," he growls. "Not until you calm the fuck down."

"You don't get to tell me what to do!" I fire back. "You deserve more than me smacking you in the face for leaving the way you did."

Jared's body stiffens. I've struck a nerve? Good. I hope so.

"I know I do." He sighs. "If I let you go, do you promise that you'll calm the fuck down so we can attempt to talk like two civilized people?"

I roll my eyes as I struggle to get out of his grasp. "A little late for talking now, don't you think?"

There's no way he can miss my pissy tone. I want him to know that I'm still angry with him after all this time. If he came here to apologize, I'm not going to make it easy on him.

"I fucked up, all right. I know that. It wasn't my intention to just come waltzing back into your life unannounced. If you give me a chance to explain myself, maybe we can actually hold a conversation without fighting." The muscles in his jaw tick beneath his skin as he blows a rush of air out through his nose. "Are you going to calm down or what?"

"I'm perfectly calm." I jerk my hands so hard that I fly backward out of his grip and slam into the corner of the door frame, nearly knocking myself out.

Jared wraps his arms around my waist and then attempts to steady me. "Easy there. Are you okay?"

"I'm fi—Ouch!" Pain rushes through my head, and I realize I may have hit it a little harder than I initially thought.

He furrows his brow, and there's a sadness in his blue eyes that I've never seen before. "I think you better sit down. Can I come in?"

I reach up and gingerly rub the spot on the back of my head that cracked against the doorjamb. I sigh and then wave him on in. "Follow me."

The clock ticking away on my living room wall is the only sound in my otherwise-silent house. Every muscle stiffens as I sit on my couch and Jared takes the seat across from me.

I study his faded blue jeans and black T-shirt, and I'm quickly reminded that anything he wears looks like a million bucks on him. He looks the same, just a little older, and there are hints of tattoos poking out from beneath his shirtsleeves.

Why are asshole men always so beautiful?

Jared tilts his head, and his blue eyes bore into me. "Are you sure you're okay?"

That voice—the one I've only heard in my dreams over the past five years—is no longer just a dream. The man it belongs to sits mere inches away from me, and I can't believe he's actually here, in my living room.

I refuse to take my eyes off him in fear that he just might disappear. "What are you doing here?"

He fidgets in his seat, wiping his hands on the thighs of his jeans as he sits in the high-backed chair across from the couch. "I didn't know this was your address, if that's what you're asking. I was doing deliveries for Mom."

I furrow my brow. "So you came here by mistake? How's that even possible when you haven't kept in touch with anyone in years?"

"I've been calling Mom, but she's the only one," he answers simply. "I also asked her not to tell you or Wes that I've been calling."

I should interrogate him on why he hadn't bothered to call me—to say something, anything, and explain why he just ran out on me like he did.

Neither of us says anything to the other, and the minutes ticking away on the clock just add to the tension. I should say something, but I'm not even sure where to start.

"I should probably get going," he says as he pushes up from his seat.

Desperation washes over me, and I know this may be my one and only shot to get some answers from Jared about things that have long haunted me.

"Wait. Please don't go." I bite my bottom lip, nervous that he'll turn and leave and I'll never get my answers—answers I've waited so long for. "Stay. Talk to me. Don't you think I at least deserve an explanation? I want to know why you pushed me away like you did. Why you wouldn't let me help you."

Pain flickers across his face, and I understand that going back to that time in his life might be painful, but it's something I need him to do. After all, he put me through hell. He owes me, and I don't feel a bit guilty making him talk to me about why he left. It might be the piece of the puzzle I've been missing to help me move on.

After a tense moment, Jared nods and then sits back down in the chair. His posture is stiff, and I can tell that he's prepared for my interrogation. "You're right. I do owe you that. Where do you want to start?"

"Okay." I blow out a slow breath between pursed lips. "Let's start with the night you came to my house drunk."

He pinches the bridge of his nose and closes his eyes. "That was one of the worst days of my life. As you know, they yanked my scholarship that day, and I went into full-on panic mode when I found out that playing ball was no longer in the cards for me. It was like everything I ever worked for—my future that I thought was set in stone—was gone. You were there for me, but I thought you deserved so much better than me at that point, and I was angry with you for lowering your standards to stand beside me. I know it sounds silly, and believe me, once I was able to think rationally about the situation, I realized what a fucked-up mental case I was that day. It was like my brain couldn't process any more.

"In Sunday school they always preached that God wouldn't give us more than we can handle, but I'm not sure how true that is. That time in my life—so much was put on me that I think it broke my rational mind. The reasoning part of my brain got buried under the anxious side that only saw the worst possibility in all situations."

I study his face, and I'm hearing what he's saying, and I believe him. I can just look into his eyes and know he's telling me the truth. It's good that he's finally able to admit how out of control he was.

"I guess what I'm saying is, the only thing left I had at that point was you. You were the one thing left in this world that could be taken from me—you and my family. I knew deep down at some point you would get tired of my shit if I could only work a minimum-wage job because I couldn't afford to finish school, and I just couldn't handle that. If I was going to lose you, I wanted it to be on my terms—that I would get rid of you first so I could avoid the blindside down the road."

"Jared . . ." I say his name in a hushed whisper. "I would've never left you. I loved you."

He stares up at me. "Something reminded me lately of how things can be taken without notice. One of my bandmates lost his mother, and it got me thinking. It's the reason I came back here. Mom won't be around forever, and I wanted to fix things between us before it was too late. I wanted to at least rectify my past with her, but you . . . I wasn't ready to face you yet."

"So you bringing the flowers . . . ?"

He shrugs one shoulder. "A simple mistake. Mom had those yellow roses set off to the side, and I grabbed them with the rest of the deliveries. I didn't know they were for you. There was no name on the card, only an address, which I thought was odd. How were you even supposed to know who they were from?"

I swallow hard. It's then that I wonder if Jared has a clue about Wes and me, because surely he would've said something about the flowers being from Wes, since he's the only person who would be sending those to me. I suddenly feel like the traitorous girlfriend, but that's ridiculous, considering I haven't seen Jared in five years. It's none of his business, really, but I should at least explain to him about the situation between Wes and me before he hears it from someone else. "I know who they're from."

He looks away from me and points his gaze down to the floor, but he doesn't look angry, more disappointed and sad. "Oh?" Jared holds his hands out in front of him, balancing his elbows on his knees, and rubs his palms together. "Are you seeing someone?"

I lick my dry lips. "It's complicated."

This was a day I never wanted to see come. Telling him—explaining why I married his brother—is something I convinced myself that I would never have to do, considering he left without a word and seemed disinterested in the things I did.

"A scorned lover then?" He raises a questioning eyebrow.

"The thing you have to understand about that is . . . well . . . it's—"

"Complicated. I got that part, and I know I have no business prying into your life. I don't have the right to do that anymore, but I can't help but be curious." There's a hint of a tease in his voice, but I know he's dying to know the answer to his questions.

I straighten my shoulders. "Let's not talk about our love lives. I'm sure mine pales in comparison to the things you've done, Mr. Rock Star."

I add the last little jab. It's way too tense in this room, and I don't think either of us is ready to unveil all our truths to one another at this point.

He smiles a bit. "You been keeping tabs on me?"

I hold up my index finger and thumb, then bring them close together, leaving only a smidgen of room between them. "Just a little. It's hard not to when I see your band everywhere I turn lately. They were just talking about your band on that gossip show *Celebrity Pop Buzz Nightly* the other night. That reporter, Linda Bronson, is determined to track down the whereabouts of your lead singer. Has he really disappeared?"

He nods. "Yeah. Our tour manager, Jane Ann, can't find him anywhere. She thinks he's gone into hiding. He's missing shows and costing Mopar Records a boatload of money. They're pretty pissed at him but are determined to find him."

"Is that why you're here?" I realize that sounds a little rude, so I try to rephrase that. "That came out wrong. What I meant to ask is, is that how you got the time off?"

"It's kind of hard to play without the band's front man," he says simply.

"I've been following your career ever since I spotted you on the band's first album cover, and I've always wondered why you weren't the lead singer. You have such an amazing voice."

He bites his bottom lip and then pulls it through his teeth. "That makes two of us. When I first signed my deal with Mopar Records, they told me that I would be the front man of the new band they were creating, and then they went out to find the rest of the band members. The moment they signed Ace, everything changed. They moved him into the front man position without talking to me about it. We showed up at our first rehearsal and it was like, surprise, meet your new lead singer."

I shake my head. "Ace is great and all, but I have to say that you are much better."

Jared smiles. "Thanks. I wish the label saw it that way."

While I know he loves being the leader, he doesn't realize that he doesn't have to be center of attention to shine. "Jared . . . I think you're already back on top. Look at what all you accomplished since you left. Music wasn't ever really your dream, just something else you were good at, and now you're so successful. Most people would kill to be in your position—people who have dreamed about it since they were kids."

He glances down at the floor like he's mulling over what I just said. Finally, after a long moment, he nods. "I sound ungrateful, don't I?"

"I didn't say that . . ."

His gaze shoots back at me. "It's okay, London. You're right, and that's one thing I need to work on. I need to find a way to accept my reality and not get upset when things get messed up."

My heart does a double thump. How I hope he means that, because the secret that I'm keeping from him is one that I hope he'll be able to accept.

"Enough about me," he says. "I want to hear about you. Looks like you're doing well."

I pick at my thumbnail. Where do I even begin? When I glance over at Jared's face, I can tell he's wondering why I'm hesitating.

He furrows his brow. "I know that look, London. What's on your mind?"

I lick my bottom lip and open my mouth, but I can't force the words to come out. This is by far the hardest thing I've ever had to do.

I close my eyes, because if I'm going to tell him this—break this secret open that I know will hurt him—there's no way I can look at him. "There's no easy way to say this . . ."

"London, I just opened up and poured my heart out to you because I want you to know how sorry I am for everything that happened. You know how fucked up I am. Whatever you're hiding can't be any worse than the shitty things I've done in my life. You can tell me. Whatever it is, I swear I won't judge you."

His words sound so sweet, and I'm convinced that he means them right now, but I know the moment he finds out about me and Wes, his niceties will fly out the window. After all, marrying his brother is the ultimate betrayal no matter how long we've been separated, but by the same token, he betrayed me too. He left me for five years without so much as a word. I can't help that the man I tried to move on with was his brother. Wes was there for me when I needed someone the most.

"Jared . . ." There's a break in my voice already, but I know this is something he needs to hear. "I—"

Before I have the chance to tell him, there's a knock on my front door. My body instantly relaxes like it's been saved by the bell.

I shove myself up from the couch. "I'll be right back."

Mentally, I scold myself for not just coming right out and telling him. After all, he walked out on me, and no matter how nice he's being to me right now, I have to keep that in the forefront of my mind.

Still going over how best to just come out with it in my head, I open the door, and the wind whooshes from my lungs. Wes stands there with his hands shoved in his pockets, and every nerve in my body panics.

There will be no gentle way of breaking the news to Jared now. Wes won't have it. He still holds so much anger toward his brother, and I know shit is about to hit the fan.

*NOW*
**JARED**

It's been five years since I've seen London, and had I known that this was her house when I grabbed the flowers off Mom's counter, I wouldn't have delivered them. I wasn't exactly ready to see her— to confess to her all my demons—but I'm glad I did. Although things are still tense, in an odd way we've fallen right back into a comfortable pattern with each other, sharing things that we can't talk to anyone else about.

Looking back, I know now that if I had just opened up to her and told her what was going on inside my head, we could've probably gotten through that dark period together. But, being the jackass I was and unable to see past my own pain, I overlooked hers. By the time I realized what I had lost when I walked out on her, it was already too late to salvage her trust in me.

When I ask her who the flowers are from, she tenses, clearly uncomfortable with telling me about that portion of her life.

Just when I think she's about to give in and tell me, the doorbell rings, and it's almost as if she's relieved.

"What are you doing here?" There's panic in her voice, and I feel like whoever sent her the flowers is here to apologize in person.

I stood up when London went to answer the door, just in case whoever it is on the other side is company that she needs to spend time with. I ready myself to leave on her command, but the voice from the other side of the door causes my back to stiffen.

"London, please. We need to talk. It's important." My brother's voice, pleading with London, makes me tilt my head.

Why is he even here?

"I told you, Wes, I need space," she tells him. "You coming around, calling, sending flowers, isn't helping."

"I'm not here because of that right now. I came to tell you that I found out that Jared is back. I felt like it was my job to warn you and come check on you."

Considering how things went the last few times I saw her, I understand Wes's concern for London. God knows I was a dick and treated her horribly, both when I left her after my fight with Wes and when she tracked me down at the bar when I was with Suzie Q's band.

"Wes," London says, "I already know."

"You do?" Even I can hear the curiosity in his voice.

I shove my hands in my pockets so I don't come off as aggressive as I step up behind London. Wes's eyes land squarely on me, and his jaw instantly stiffens. Clearly there won't be one of those made-for-television reunion moments happening between my brother and me. The expression on his face tells me that he's pissed that I'm here.

"You've got to be kidding me," Wes growls as he redirects his gaze back to London. "You let him in here? Have you lost your mind?"

"Wes, please," she pleads. "Calm down. We're just talking."

"I won't calm down! He doesn't get to talk to you—not after what he did—not ever! The bastard doesn't deserve any kindness from you."

I understand why he's mad, but he's got to be able to tell by looking at me that I am not the same hothead I was before. I need to make him understand that I mean her no harm. "Wes, man, look, I know—"

He points his finger in my direction. "You can just shut up. Whatever you think you had with her in the past, it's over. You blew your chances with her."

"If I want to talk to her, you can't stop me," I retort. "It's up to her if she wants me to leave or not. This is her house."

Wes narrows his eyes at me. "That's where you're wrong again. This is my house, asshole."

I flinch. "Your house?" My eyes flick down to London. "What's he talking about?"

She swallows hard. "That's what I was trying to tell you before. Wes and I . . ."

I hold my breath as she struggles to tell me exactly what's going on between them. My heart squeezes in my chest, and my knees grow a little weak after my brain puts two and two together.

Unable to wait on her to finish, I fill in the gap. "The two of you live together? You're like a thing?"

"We're more than a 'thing.' London is my wife."

My eyes widen and it's suddenly hard to breathe. *"Wife . . . ?"*

"That's right. Things have changed since you walked out of here, so don't act so surprised that she moved on without you. You left her for five years! I was the one who stayed and picked up all the pieces of the mess you left behind. So like I said, you don't get to talk to her. She no longer belongs to you."

My eyes widen. All of the times when I was out on the road touring and thought about London and my family, never did I picture this scenario happening. Sure, I knew Wes had a thing for

London, but I didn't think London would ever reciprocate Wes's feelings. She always seemed so oblivious to the way he looked at her.

Ever since we were kids, I noticed Wes stared at London a little too long, but I couldn't blame him. London is the most beautiful girl I've ever seen. It's hard to not notice her.

The rage I normally feel when things don't go my way isn't there. I've learned too much about how much hurt flying off the handle can cause. Them being together—it's my fault. Leaving did push them together. I have no doubt that my brother was probably the shoulder she cried on when I shattered her heart.

Wes is right. I no longer have any claim on London. I left her behind—walked completely out of her life—it's not fair of me to be upset that she moved on.

I close my eyes and frown. When I reopen them, I flick my gaze from London to my brother and then back again, knowing this whole situation was created by me. I can't be mad at them. More than anything, I envy Wes. He has the life that I wanted with London, living the dream that I screwed up when I walked out on her.

I swallow hard. "I'm sorry."

Wes's head snaps back a bit, and he furrows his brow. This wasn't the answer that he was expecting. "Why are you sorry?"

"For causing all this. We never used to fight like this. We all just got along, but now . . . I deserve this. I might as well have pushed the two of you together myself."

"Jared . . ." London's eyes glisten with tears.

"It's okay, London. I understand. He loves you—he always has. I'm glad there was someone there for you when I left."

She shakes her head. "That's not how it happened. We just started officially seeing each other a year ago, and our marriage . . . it's not working."

"It's not working because you can't get over him and what he did to you." Wes points at me. "You love him way more than he deserves."

The hurt in Wes's voice is clear. The tension between these two still seems raw from the outside of the situation, and I seem to be the very source of what's ruining their marriage. It's time for me to leave before I make things any worse for them. "I'm just going to go. The two of you obviously have a lot that you need to work out."

Wes steps back, allowing me to pass by him. "Yeah, I think it's best you go."

The coldness in his voice stings as I walk out onto the porch, leaving Wes and London behind. The closeness I once shared with my brother is long gone. I don't see a way back to the relationship we once had, since it's clear that we're both in love with the same woman.

"Jared, don't go!" London pleads. "Stay."

I turn around and face her. "I'm sorry, London. I don't belong here. You and Wes . . ." I hesitate, unsure of what to say. "You don't need me in the middle of this, causing you any more problems."

I don't give her a chance to say anything else. I all but run to the delivery van, jump inside, and speed off to process everything I've just learned. Once the initial shock passes, grief washes over me. The relationship I had with London is dead and gone, and it hits home that I've really lost her. Even though I'm the one who left her, a small glimmer of hope always flickered in the back of my mind that someday, somehow, we'd find our way back to one another. But now she's with Wes, my own brother. It's ironic that I expected Wes to stay out of my relationship with London, and now the shoe is on the other foot.

She said things between them weren't working out, but I won't intrude on their marriage. I can't interfere no matter how bad I want her back. I've already been selfish enough when it comes to Wes and London, and I don't want to hurt either of them any more.

When I get back to the shop, Mom greets me with a smile. "How'd it go?"

I smile but decide that I'm not ready to tell her about who I just ran into. "It was fine."

She frowns, and I'm sure she already knows that I took the yellow roses and delivered them to London, but she's not letting on that she does. I know my mother, and she's waiting on me to dive into telling her the bad news before bringing it up herself.

"No problems? And you found everyone all right?" she asks again.

I nod. "Everything went fine." I need a distraction. "Are you ready for dinner? I'm starving."

Mom wipes her hands on the faded blue towel she's holding. "Yep. All done here. Let's go."

Through dinner, I'm quiet. It's not that I don't want to talk to Mom and hear all about what's been going on in her life, it's just that I can't stop thinking about Wes and London.

Mom reaches across the table and places her hand on my forearm. "Is everything okay? You seem like your mind is somewhere else."

I take a drink from my water glass and sigh. I could continue to hide the fact that I know about London and Wes, but my mind is teetering with so many questions. Who better to ask than her? "Why didn't you tell me about the wedding?"

Her lips pull into a tight line, and then she sighs. "I thought you took the yellow roses."

I nod. "I did, and let me tell you, I don't know who was shocked more—me or London."

"I can imagine. I never meant for you to find out that way. My plan was to break the news to you once we came here for dinner. How are you doing now that you know?"

I shrug. "I think I'm still in shock. Honestly, I can't believe London married my brother. It just hurts so damn bad. I wanted to marry her. I wanted to be the one who gave her the Kraft name, but I wasn't here to do that. It's my fault that they're together, and I can't even be mad at them, even though I wish I were. It would be a whole lot easier to hate them both instead of having this heart-wrenching sadness inside me right now."

"*Were* together," Mom corrects. "They were only married about three months, and London broke it off."

I stare at Mom from across the table, and I can see the wheels turning in her brain. She wants me to know that Wes and London are over, and it's almost as if she's trying to encourage me to not give up hope of getting London back. But the thing is, even if she somehow finds a spot in her heart that still loves me and is able to forgive me—us being together, it will crush Wes.

"I don't understand why it had to be him. Of all the guys in the world, she had to marry Wes. The biggest question on my mind is why."

Mom sighs. "The thing you have to understand, son, is that London was so in love with you that when you left it nearly broke her. She tried to be strong and pretend that she was coping with everything, but I could tell that she was lost without you. Now, Wes is my son, and I love him dearly, but he knew how London felt about you, and he pursued her anyway. I warned him to stop—that she was still stuck on you—but he refused to give up, and eventually that persistence wore London down. It's hard not to feel something for the man who has been by your side constantly for the last five years while you went through a soul-crushing experience. Wes was that for her—there for her. He comforted her through the darkest times of her life. When she finally gave in and began to date him, I knew it would never last, even if my own son couldn't see it. London was, and still is, too hung up on you to let someone else into her heart right now. Wes never had a chance with her."

This was a new revelation. "You think she still loves me? Even after the hell I put her through—what I put all of you through?"

"I do," she says simply. "Every time I talk to the girl, she asks if I've heard from you . . . even after all this time. It was hard to keep the fact that I was talking to you secret from her because I know how much she worries about you."

I scrub my hand down my face. "This whole thing is so screwed up, Mom. How am I ever supposed to right so many wrongs?"

"Do you still love her?" Mom asks.

The answer to her question is an obvious yes. "Of course I do. Protecting her from the evil that was growing inside me is the whole reason I left. I tried to outrun myself and stay out of touch because I didn't want to bring Wes or London down with me. It was self-ish of me, but I did that because I loved her. I needed to get myself back under control before I could be good enough for her again."

"Were you able to tell her how you feel when you saw her today?"

"No. We talked a bit, but Wes showed up pretty quickly after we started talking, and telling someone that you still have feelings for them after running out on them five years ago isn't something you can just blurt out."

I sigh. If I had been better prepared to face her, maybe I would've had a speech planned out to tell her exactly how I feel. I wish I had known the situation before walking into it. "How could you not have told me about London and Wes?"

Mom frowns and her blue eyes appear sad. "You would get angry with me and cut our call short any time I even mentioned her name. There was no way I could ever even entertain the idea of telling you that they got married, especially over the phone. I was afraid it would drive you even further away. I know you were dealing with a lot. Dad . . ." She trails off, and I can tell it's still pretty tough for her to talk about him. "Him dying, that was so unexpected. We all had to deal with it in our own way, and I just knew you weren't in the right frame of mind to handle any more heartbreaking news, so I kept it from you. I apologize for that. I just did what I thought was best for you. Please don't be upset with me. I can't take losing you over this."

I still have a hard time dealing with the loss of Dad myself, but keeping in contact with Mom and paying tribute to him through the love of music we shared helped me to heal. I'm still not over Dad's death, but I can at least hear his name and think about him without falling completely apart.

She's right. As much as I hate to admit it, she's right. If I had found out that London and Wes had gotten married, there would be no way in hell I would've even considered coming back here. The thought of the two of them together, touching, kissing, and having sex . . . Goddamn, that one stings like fire. To know that he's held her in his arms and made love to her . . . the thought alone is almost more than I can take.

I am such a fucking idiot. How could I have done this? Driven a wedge between us like this? Running away caused all this, and the only way I can make things better between me and my family is to make sure that I don't disappear again.

"I'm not going anywhere." I reach over and squeeze Mom's hand to reassure her a bit.

The moment London opened the door and my eyes fell upon her, my heart stopped beating for a moment. I knew without a shadow of a doubt that I was still in love with this woman. Seeing her in person reignited every ounce of love I ever had for her.

As if Mom is reading my thoughts, she says, "If you still feel something for her, you must tell her. The girl has been miserable without you, and if she doesn't get some type of closure with you, I'm not sure if she'll ever be able to truly move on."

I take in her words, and I know deep down that she's right. London needs to know how I feel. I need to at least attempt to right the wrongs I've caused and give London the closure that she needs from me if being with Wes is what truly makes her happy now. It will kill me knowing she's with my brother, but Wes and London deserve to be happy.

### THEN
### LONDON

**S**am waves the bag of doughnuts around in my face. "You know you want one."

I groan and pull the covers back over my face. "Go away with your evil, fatty goodness."

"No way. Don't even try that. You, missy, are all skin and bones. A doughnut or ten will not kill you. Now, sit your pretty ass up and eat."

I hate when she gets like this, but it's also what makes me love her even more. She's persistent and pushy in the best kind of loving way, and there's no getting out of whatever it is that she's asking of you when she's in full-on mother hen mode.

"Don't make me call Wes over here," Sam threatens. "Seems like he's the only one who can convince you to do anything lately, which is odd, considering that his brother is the reason you live like a hermit."

I sit up and grab the bag. "Please don't call him. I don't think I can take him right now."

"Lovers' quarrel?" Sam teases, and I roll my eyes.

"It's not like that between us. You know that. He's just been my rock over the past few years since Jared left."

"I'll bet he has. You would think since you were his brother's fiancée that you'd be off limits to him, but the boy doesn't seem to respect that boundary at all. He's got it bad for you."

I shake my head. "No, he doesn't."

Sam plops down beside me and tosses her blond hair over one shoulder. "I love you, London, but sometimes you really are blind. Wes obviously loves you, and who knows, maybe it would be good for you to try dating him, since he's the only member of the male species besides your dad that you'll speak with. It might pull you out of this funk."

"I don't think about him that way. He's just a really good friend."

"A *really* hot good friend," she teases, and when I don't laugh or roll my eyes at her joke so that she knows I'm not amused, she throws her arm around me. "Okay, so you *don't* have feelings for him that way. I get it. But I want you to be aware that he does feel like that toward you, and I don't want you to string him along forever if you have no intentions of dating him. Put the poor guy out of his misery."

I completely hear what she's saying. I don't want to be one of those girls who leads a guy on, but I also don't want to lose Wes either.

This isn't something I want to think about right now. It scares me to know that there's a possibility that Wes won't be in my life at some point. I need to change the subject.

"Speaking of misery, so I have to go on this blind date with you tonight?" I whine.

"Yes! I don't do first dates with a guy I met at a party alone. You know that. I need my wing woman, and you have to go out with what I'm sure is Josh's delectable friend to help me out."

I laugh. "If he's not delectable, then you're going to owe me big time."

She smiles. "I'll just keep bribing you with doughnuts."

Later that night we pull up in front of this local pool hall we hang out in from time to time called The Station, there to meet Josh and this mystery date. The parking lot is packed, and the same goes for inside the smoke-filled bar. Bodies fill every inch of the place just like any other Saturday night, and I begin searching faces in the crowd in order to locate Josh.

"Oh, there they are," Sam says as she points toward the back of the bar.

My eyes zero in on the direction her finger motioned to, and, finally, I spot Josh standing there with a pool stick in his hand, leaning against the wall. Curiosity as to what my date looks like fills my mind, and my eyes instantly flit over to the guy Josh is standing next to. The moment my eyes land on a familiar face, my mouth falls agape.

I grab Sam's arm, halting her from going any farther. "Hold up. My date is Wes? Are you kidding me? I could strangle you right now for not warning me about this. You know I'm not ready for this."

Sam twists her pouty pink lips. "He loves you, London, and he's a nice guy. Give him a shot."

I fold my arms over my chest, silently stewing and debating turning around and walking right back out the door.

Sam's shoulders slump when she sees I'm not pleased about this. "Look, London, I didn't mean to piss you off. You're my best friend, and my heart breaks every time I watch you cry over Jared. Think of this as a lovin' push toward possible happiness."

I sigh. How can I be pissed at her when it's obvious that her sneaking around and plotting behind my back came from a good place? While my love for Wes isn't anything romantic, maybe someday it could be if I figure out a way to let go. I owe it to him and myself to see if being with him can help me find happiness again.

I glance back in Josh's direction, and he elbows Wes and then points to where Sam and I are standing. A bashful smile fills Wes's face, and he slowly lifts his hand and mouths the word "hi" to me.

I hook my arm through Sam's and decide that now is the time to open myself up to taking a chance on a new direction in my life. "Okay."

Sam smiles at me, and I can tell she's pleased that I'm giving in. "Let's go have some fun."

Six months after the night Sam and Josh set me up on the blind date with Wes, I find myself standing on the stage in a church. I watch the door in the back of the room just as anxiously as Josh, waiting for a girl who means so much to each of us. When the "Wedding March" finally plays, everyone in the room stands up, and the door finally opens, revealing Sam, who looks more beautiful than ever.

With her arm tucked tightly under her dad's, Sam makes her way down the aisle, taking care to not trip over her dress and fall. Most people in this room don't know it, but Sam is working on her fourth month of pregnancy, and with the war still in full swing, Josh thought enlisting in active duty would be a good way to support his little family. He ships out in two weeks, and Sam and he planned this wedding on the fly to ensure they get the full benefits package that the army provides.

Sam's dad hands her off to Josh, and the pastor informs everyone that they may be seated. I stand next to my best friend on the most important day of her life as she marries the man that she loves wholeheartedly.

It's times like these that make me think of Jared, since our plan was to get married someday.

It makes me wonder if this would have been us, standing in a church, professing our love for all to see. I've noticed with all the time I've spent helping Sam plan her wedding that I've been thinking more and more crazy things like this lately.

I stare down at Wes, who sits on a pew next to my dad, and when he catches me looking at him, he smiles. Wes and I have been together nearly every day since Sam forced me to open my eyes that night at the pool hall and see that Wes really cares about me. Other than Sam, he is my closest friend, and I don't know what I would've done without him over the past couple of years. He's really helped me hold everything together. I think in large part it's just the fact that he knows what I've been through, and why I'm not ready to date again, that has helped a lot. He knows how much I loved his brother and knows that I struggle each and every day to forget about him and just move on, without much success.

Since it's obvious to me now that Wes wants more than friendship with me, I've tried to be more conscious about not leading him on. I tried to distance myself from him and not depend on him so much, but he makes it pretty damn easy to lean on him when I need support.

"You may now kiss your bride," the pastor says, causing a huge smile to erupt on Josh's face, and he leans in and cups Sam's face before planting a kiss square on her lips. We all cheer as they turn and face the congregation. "May I present to you Mr. and Mrs. Joshua Clayborn."

Music plays and they walk out, and I follow them, wondering if this will ever be me someday. I know Wes is in love with me, but

I'm still hesitant to take things to the next level . . . but maybe some-day. The best I can hope for is that I will find a man who loves me enough to want to make me his forever at some point—one who will love me as much as I do him. I thought I found that once with Jared. I was wrong, but I'm still determined to not give up on love, and I pray that one day it finds me again.

**A**loud chirp sounds as a text hits my cell while I sit at a red light. I glance at my phone and am surprised to see it's from Julie, and she wants me to come over to her place to talk. Ever since Wes and I have separated, I have purposefully stayed away from her. It's too hard to look at her and know that I'm hurting her Wes, and I've not been ready to face her just yet.

Almost as if she can sense my reservation, a second text comes through: *Please.*

I sigh, knowing that it's time to sit down and talk to the woman who's been like a second mother to me ever since I lost my own.

A horn blares behind me, and I head to Dad's house, since he's right down the street. When I pull up against the curb out front of Dad's and get out of the car, I glance toward the Kraft house and notice Jared out front mowing his mother's lawn.

I can't take my eyes off Jared as he works. It's like we're magnets, and I'm drawn to him whether I want to be or not. I twirl my car keys in my fingers and then walk down the sidewalk toward him.

Sun shines down on his shirtless back, and I watch his muscles work beneath his skin as he pushes the machine over the green blades of grass. His blue jeans hug his backside perfectly.

I forgot how unbelievably sexy he is without his shirt on. When he rounds the corner, he notices me standing on the sidewalk watching him, so he cuts the engine on the mower.

He squints one eye like he's trying to block out the sun. "London?"

I glance nervously to the driveway and notice Julie's car isn't there.

I raise my hand up in greeting. "Hey. Do you know that time your mom will be home from the shop? She asked me to stop by so we could talk about something, but now I can't reach her because the battery on my cell died."

He pulls a shirt from his back pocket and wipes his face but doesn't bother putting it back on. "No idea. Do you want to come in and try her cell?"

I nod, standing there ogling the perfectly toned, tattooed male body in front of me. "Yeah. That would be great."

He motions me toward the house and then follows me up the stoop. I can feel his blue eyes boring into my backside. Knowing that he's checking me out makes me feel desired.

"Phone is on the counter." Jared walks into the kitchen and washes his hands. "Do you want something to drink? I bought some beer last night."

"Yeah, that would—" I quickly stop myself. I don't need to sit and casually drink with the man that I lust after most. I need to keep a clear head around him so I don't do something stupid. "Just some water would be fine."

The cabinet doors creak open and then slam shut as he grabs a glass and goes to the refrigerator to use the ice maker. "So what's going on?"

I bite the inside of my cheek. "I'm not sure. She just texted me and asked me to stop by and chat."

He chews his bottom lip. "That's odd, considering she just left here about thirty minutes ago and told me she was meeting the ladies from her book club for dinner. The way she talked, she'll be gone for quite a while."

He hands me the glass of ice water. "Thank you." I take a small sip. "Do you know how long you'll be sticking around?"

Jared pops the top off a beer and then leans back against the counter. "I'm not sure. I guess I'm off until our lead singer decides to come out of hiding, which I'm hoping is soon, considering that we don't get paid if we don't play any gigs. Record sales barely make any money these days. It's all about touring."

"Makes sense, I guess, but that sucks for you."

He smiles. "Tell me about it. My job as a musician is so uncertain. It's not like we have a retirement plan, but it's nice that I'm able to invest a lot while the money is rolling in."

"You sound a lot like your dad when you say stuff like that," I tell him, but grimace because I'm sure that's still a very sore subject for him.

He gives me a closed-mouth smile. "Thanks. I wish he was here now. There are so many things I want to talk to him about."

"That's how I feel about my mom. There are days—like today— that I miss her so bad. It would be so much easier if I could just pick up the phone and call her—ask for her advice."

He nods. "That's exactly how I feel."

I open my mouth to say more about Henry but hold back because I don't want to push the subject too far and make Jared uncomfortable. So far he seems very calm and rational—a far cry from five years ago.

I bite my lip but then decide to just continue bringing up his father to gauge where he's at emotionally with his father's death, because last time I saw him he couldn't handle it. "I really loved Henry. He was like a father to me too, so I understand why you lost it the way you did after he passed. He was pretty amazing."

"That he was," Jared says softly as he stares into my eyes. It seems that he has no trouble talking about his dad now.

He sighs. "I was wrong for taking off the way I did, London. I've apologized to Mom I don't know how many times, but I'm so sorry that it took me until recently to tell you that. I loved you so much, and you don't know how bad I wish that I'd never screwed things up between us. I would say that I wish I could have a second chance to prove to you how much you mean to me and how I would never leave you like I did before, but I know that's not fair of me to say. You're with Wes now, and I have to learn to deal with that."

Tears burn my eyes. "You don't know how bad I wish that too, but you hurt me so much. I cried for you—still do. You completely wrecked me. Wes and I—it just sort of happened. I was lonely and he was there for me through a really dark period in my life. I never meant for me and Wes—"

He steps to me and presses his index finger to my lips. "Don't. You don't have to be sorry for that. I wasn't there for you, and Wes was. I understand why you gave it a shot with him."

I stare at him in amazement. This wasn't the reaction I expected from him. The old Jared would've been angry with me no matter how many times I apologized for marrying his brother. This new side of him seems to understand and has compassion for the mistake I made, which only makes me explain how I still feel about him.

"He reminded me so much of you. The things that attracted me to him pushed me away at the same time. Every day I was with him,

I thought of you. Being around him reminded me of what I lost with you. Wes knew it—but he loved me anyway. I just couldn't love him back in the same way—not the way I loved you. You were it for me, and that's why things were doomed from the start with Wes and me."

He cups my face. "London . . ."

"Jared." I can only whisper his name in return before he pulls me in for a kiss.

He doesn't move too fast. He holds my face in his hands as he presses his mouth to mine. There's no urgency in his actions. It's almost as if he's taking the time to savor every second of this.

He wraps his arms around my waist and pulls me in tighter. "I've missed you so much. Can you ever forgive me for leaving you—for that night in the parking lot? For everything? You should hate me, I know that, but I swear to God if you'll let me, I'll make it up to you."

For years I've dreamed of him saying this, begging for my forgiveness and promising that he would make it up to me. I know I should hate him and not give in so easy, but I'd be lying if I said I didn't want this so bad. I still love him, and I need to know that I can trust him again and that his intentions with my heart are pure.

I lean my forehead against his. "God, I want to believe that, but I'm scared. I can't take you crushing my heart again."

He squeezes his eyes shut like it pains him to look at me, and then he opens them and pulls back to meet my gaze head-on. "I deserve that. God knows I did you wrong. Please give me a shot. I'll understand if you guard your heart for a while until I can prove to you that I'm deserving of it."

Jared cups my face. "You're *my* girl, London. There's no one else but you, and never has been, and I'll love you until my very last day on this earth."

I stare into his blue eyes and then touch his bottom lip with my thumb. "I want this with you so much."

"I want you too, but I want to know that I'm your choice. That you and Wes—that whatever that was between the two of you is over. Finished. I need that peace of mind before we go any further."

I can see the pleading in his eyes for the permission he needs to claim me as his own again. I bite my bottom lip as I speak the truth out loud. "Wes and I were over before we ever began. It's you that I love, Jared. It always has been."

Jared smiles as he grips my hips and lifts me up to the counter with ease before hitching my legs around his waist. "You don't know how happy that makes me to hear you say that. I swear, I'll never leave your side again. Not ever."

I melt into his words. They mean so much to me. I've wanted to hear them for so long, and I can't help but give in to the moment and kiss him with all my might. This, in turn, excites him. Jared's hands are everywhere, tugging on my clothes in order to get his hands onto my bare skin. When he threads his fingers into my hair, he pulls me deeper into his kiss. This is the ultimate way to make a woman feel desired—to act like you can't get enough of her and want her so much you can barely stand it. I absolutely love the way it makes me feel.

His hands settle on my hips as he pulls me even closer, pushing himself between my legs. The shorts I'm wearing creep up my thighs and stretch across the skin of my legs. His lips attack mine, and I find myself completely immersed in him.

I adjust my hips and feel the hard cock in his jeans rub up against me. No man has ever been able to arouse me this much. There's something about Jared that attracts me, and I'm drawn to him no matter what bad shit he's done. The way he so blatantly wants me— the way he's laid it all out there on the line—is a complete turn-on.

"God, London, I've missed this—us—so much. No other woman holds my heart, never has. Only you," Jared says. "I'm so sorry for what I've done. So sorry."

He keeps chanting those words softly in my ear, over and over. Every instinct inside me tells me that he means it, which only reignites all the old feelings that I had for him, bringing them all to the forefront in full force.

It's always been Jared who's owned my heart. Wes has only been a crutch—someone I used to convince myself that I was over Jared. All those nights lying awake and wondering where Jared was and if he was thinking about me, I've finally gotten my answer. He was dreaming of me too.

The heat of his stare overwhelms me as he pulls back and then presses his lips to mine. My panties grow wet, and I'm so turned on by finally being in his arms again that I can't see straight.

Dear God. I can't believe he's gotten even sexier with time.

"I want you so much," he whispers before kissing the sensitive flesh below my ear. "Tell me you want me too."

Those words flowing from his lips cause the rational side of my brain to shut down completely and allow my greedy body to take control of my actions.

I grab his face and crush my lips to his. My fingers find their way into his thick, dark hair as I hold him in place while he returns my kiss with such passion that I'm sure my panties are about to ignite.

My hands roam over the rigid muscles of Jared's rock-hard abs before I grind my pelvis against him.

When my eyes drift down to his body, I lick my lips in anticipation. The pronounced "V" of his hips points like an arrow at what I know is a considerable length hiding behind those jeans.

I move my hand down to the button of his fly while he pulls my blouse over my head. He dips his head down to the tops of my breasts. He drags his lips over the mounded flesh as he works my white, lacey bra down to expose my puckered nipples.

"You are so perfect," Jared murmurs before sucking one of my nipples into his mouth.

We tear away each other's clothing, but it's like we can't get each other naked fast enough. The sounds of both of us panting fill the room while we take turns licking, kissing, and tasting one another.

Jared drags my panties down my legs and then shoves his underwear down too, clearing away all things from between us.

He hooks his arms under my thighs and pulls my hips to the edge of the counter before he uses his fingers to splay open my most sensitive flesh and rub my clit.

I writhe against the palm of his hand and my head drops back. "Jared . . ." I say his name like a plea. It's been far too long since I've experienced such pleasure that I don't want it to end.

Saying his name only causes his finger to move faster, circling and teasing me, causing that familiar euphoric feeling of an impending orgasm to rush through my body.

Every nerve ending in me ignites as I let loose and fall into the bliss of pure ecstasy.

His lips connect with mine and our mouths meld together. I've missed this—I've missed him so damn much.

I press my pussy against his crotch and rub myself against his cock. "I want you."

He inhales sharply through his nose and then blows his hot breath across my lips. "God, I want you too. So much."

Jared bites his lip as I reach between us, eager to touch and explore his beautiful body. His flesh is warm and silky as I wrap my fingers around his shaft and guide it to my entrance.

"Shit," he murmurs as he licks his lips, and then he brings his face back up so he can stare at me with his lust-coated eyes. He reaches out and flicks his thumb over my still-erect nipple.

I bite my lip as I inch closer to the edge of the counter, guiding his cock up and down my folds, making impact with my clit each time.

Jared sucks a quick breath through his teeth. "Jesus. You're so fucking wet."

He crushes his mouth to mine as he thrusts his hips forward, and just the tip of his cock slides inside me. I spread my legs wider and grab his ass in both of my hands. "I want you inside me."

He trails his nose along my jawline. "You don't know how bad I want to fuck you. I've thought about you for so long. I know once I'm inside of you that I won't last. I want you too damn much."

"Please," I beg. "Make me feel good," I whisper against his lips.

As soon as the words fall from my lips, he thrusts his cock inside me, and I clench down around him.

"Fuck," he breathes, moving at a deliciously slow pace. He drops his head and rests his forehead on my shoulder. "You—God, you're amazing. I don't want this to end."

"Oh, you feel so good," I tell him as he moves a little faster. "Harder," I tell him, feeling a little greedy as I seek out another orgasm.

He snakes his arms under mine and splays his hands on my back as he does exactly as I ask.

"*Yes,*" I hiss.

That familiar tingle erupts throughout my body as he drives himself inside me.

I pant, and my mouth drifts open as I come again. "Oh, God. Jared, yes!"

"Come for me, baby. You're so fucking sexy," he growls as I come undone under him.

He thrusts into me a few more times before he curses and comes inside me. He stills and then pulls out, rubbing his come-covered cock over my folds.

He bites his bottom lip. "I'm sorry about that. I should've used a condom, but I was so caught up. I want you to know that I'm clean, I get tested regularly. You're still on the pill, right?"

I shake my head. I should've stopped him, but my stupid body just doesn't know how to say no when it comes to this man.

Jared sighs and then jams his fingers into his hair. "If something happens, we'll handle it, okay? I promise you can count on me now."

I pull back and stare into his blue eyes. "Jared . . ." I say his name almost like a whisper.

He furrows his brow. "I know that look, London. What's wrong?"

I open my mouth to answer him, but a wave of nausea hits me hard, and I twist just in time to vomit into the kitchen sink.

"Oh my God. London? Are you all right?" There's thick concern in Jared's voice as he stands behind me and holds my hair back while I continue to expel my lunch. "Why didn't you tell me you weren't feeling well?"

I shake my head. "I didn't feel sick until just a few seconds ago. It was like I just got off of an amusement park ride and the world was still spinning."

"So you're saying I just rocked your world?" I can hear the teasing in his voice, and I reach behind me to smack him. "Ouch. Kidding. Only kidding."

I turn the faucet on and rinse the contents in the sink down the drain and then cup my hand to fill it with water to wash my mouth out. When I stand up, Jared watches me closely, like I'm a puking time bomb that's ready to erupt again at any second.

He hands me a paper towel. "You okay?"

I take it and wipe my face. "Yeah. I'm okay."

"Does that happen often, or is it just sex with me that makes you ill?"

I roll my eyes. "I'm not sure what happened. I was fine before and during. It was . . . I don't know."

Jared's lips twist. "Maybe you should go to Dr. Friedman and get it checked out."

I nod. "Maybe I will."

Jared bites his lip. "I'll go with you, if you want. His office had the best suckers."

I laugh, finding it amusing that he remembers that about the family doctor both he and I have gone to since we were in junior high school. "I think I can handle going to the doctor on my own, but I'll be sure to tell him how big of a fan you are of his treats."

The next day I sit in the waiting room of my family doctor as I listen for my name to be called. I've felt sick for the last month, but I chalked it up to being stressed over the separation in my marriage. Puking for no apparent reason is definitely a new thing.

Jared showing up two days ago has made things worse. Being caught between two men has magnified my stress levels tenfold. I've decided it's time to get checked and get a prescription for nerve pills if that's what I need. After I left Jared yesterday, I couldn't stop replaying what occurred between us in that kitchen. I'm not sure where we go from here. I would love nothing more than to try and start over with him. Jared and I need to sit down and figure out this thing between us.

"London Kraft," the short, dark-haired nurse in blue scrubs calls from the doorway.

I toss the magazine I was reading back down on the table in front of me and push up out of the chair. "That's me."

I follow her down the hallway. After she asks me why I'm here, she weighs me and takes my blood pressure, and then ushers me into a small exam room. "The doctor will be right in."

Nearly twenty minutes later, Dr. Anthony Friedman comes waltzing in the door. Dr. Friedman always looks exactly the same every time I come in here. Hair combed over to the side and thick-framed glasses complement his white lab coat, completing the stereotypical nerdy appearance.

He sits down at the small desk in the room with what I assume is my chart in his hand. "So, London, my nurse says you're not feeling well—some general tiredness and nausea. Is there anything else going on?"

"Those are the main things," I tell him. "I've never felt so off before in my life."

He glances down at the chart. "And you've been feeling this way for nearly a month?" I nod and he makes a note. "When was your last menstrual period?"

I furrow my brow as I try to remember. I've been so distracted lately that I can't recall. "I'm not sure."

Dr. Friedman's eyes soften. "Let's get a pregnancy test for you, and we'll start from there."

My stomach drops to the floor, and a wave of nausea rolls over me. Is this really happening to me right now? I rub my forehead and then close my eyes.

I guess it is possible that I might be pregnant. Wes and I didn't use birth control—messing around with my hormones made me too weepy—but I did keep track of when I ovulate so that we could avoid sex around those times. We haven't been married long enough to even entertain the idea of starting a family.

When Dr. Friedman leaves the room, the dark-haired nurse pokes her head back through the door. "London, if you'll come with me over to the restroom."

I follow her but am in full-on robot mode, just going through the motions. I chew the meaty flesh on the inside of my bottom lip, trying to hide the fact that my heart is beating a thousand miles a minute inside my chest as I try not to freak the fuck out until I know if I'm pregnant or not.

She opens the door to the restroom and hands me plastic cup that has my name on it. "Fill it up to the line and then open the little door on the wall and set it inside. Any questions?"

"No," I whisper.

After I provide the sample, she sticks me back into the exam room, where I wait for what feels like forever for the doctor to come back in and give me the results.

Dr. Friedman sits back down at the little desk across from me. "Congratulations, you're pregnant."

My eyes widen, and I suck in a quick breath. "Are you sure?"

I clutch my chest at the realization of how this will affect getting back together with Jared. It can never happen now—not after this.

He nods. "Our tests are pretty accurate, but of course, we always do a full blood workup too. Since you can't remember the date of your last menstrual period, there's no way to know for sure exactly how far along you are. You'll need to make an appointment with an OB to confirm the pregnancy, and if you need help finding one, let my staff in the front office know, and they can help you. In the meantime, I'm going to write you a one-month supply of prenatal vitamins and advise you to start eating healthy. Follow the basic food groups, limit your caffeine intake, and absolutely no alcohol. Any questions?"

My entire body is numb, and while I'm sure I'll have a million questions later on, I can't think of a single one right now. The only thing that's on my mind is telling Jared.

I stare up at the doctor and do my best to fight back tears as I shake my head.

"I know this is a lot to take in, especially if you weren't trying to get pregnant. Go home and talk about this with your partner, and I'm sure that will help."

I walk out of that office completely stunned with a handful of pamphlets and my first OB appointment. The idea of a baby and having a family of my own is something I've always dreamed about, but I never planned on things happening like this. This isn't the most opportune time to bring a life into this world, considering Wes and I are separated and I don't see any way of fixing our marriage. What in the hell am I going to do? When Wes finds out about this baby, he's going to fight like hell to make our marriage work.

When I reach my car, there's only one person I can think of to speak with about this situation—the one person who I know I'm about to lose again.

*NOW*
## LONDON

I park in front of Julie's house and take a deep breath, feeling thankful that Julie isn't home for this conversation I'm about to have with her son. Of all the scenarios I've ever pictured in my head when I think about Jared, walking in to tell him that I'm pregnant with his brother's baby isn't one of them.

I hop out of the car and make my way up the sidewalk of the little blue house while dread creeps over me. I don't know how I'm supposed to break this to him. Hell, I haven't even fully processed this myself.

I knock on the door, and I hear movement on the other side. When Jared opens it, he grins and his beautiful blue eyes sparkle with excitement.

"London." He says my name with what sounds like a relieved sigh as his strong, tattooed arms wrap around me. "I've missed you."

I pull back and open my mouth but then quickly close it as tears stream down my face. Confusion washes over Jared's face as he leads me into the house and closes the door behind us. I can tell that he's concerned, but he doesn't say anything for a long minute.

I stare up into his eyes, and suddenly I know it will kill me to tell him what I've just discovered.

When I try to turn away, Jared grabs my waist and halts me from leaving.

Jared bites his bottom lip as he cradles my face in his hands and I hold on to his back. "Tell me, please," he begs. "Whatever it is—we'll get through this. Let me be there for you."

"I . . ." I pause as every nerve in my body begins to jitter. It's so wrong of me to even entertain the idea of telling Jared about the baby before Wes knows, but I feel like he needs to know. He needs to know the reason that I can't be with him and why this time it's me walking out of his life forever.

If I thought telling him I married his brother was hard, telling him I am carrying his brother's baby is going to gut me, but this is one secret that I can't hide from him. "I'm pregnant."

All of the muscles in his back tense under my fingers. He slowly pulls back. "That's why you were sick yesterday?"

I nod. "Yes. I just came from the doctor. I thought it was stress and that I was just on the verge of having a mental breakdown with everything going on—the divorce, you—but that wasn't the case. They did a urine test and told me that I wasn't sick, just pregnant."

He rakes his hand through his hair. "Does Wes know?"

I shake my head. "No, and I know as soon as he finds out, he's going to push even harder for us to be together."

"And you don't want that?"

"No," I whisper.

He licks his lips. "Then what do you want?"

*You!* I want to scream out, but I know deep down that I can't do that. It wouldn't be right to do this to Wes. Even though Wes doesn't own my heart, I know this baby will, and I'll do whatever it takes to make him or her happy. "What I want is what's best for this baby, and it's going to need its father."

He sighs and then brushes a strand of my dark hair off my cheek. "London . . ." He trails off, and I can tell there's so much that he wants to say, but he stops himself. "I know how much a father means to a little kid." He closes his eyes, and his Adam's apple bobs when he swallows hard before he opens them again and stares into my eyes. He furrows his brow, and I can tell he's doing his best to hide just how crushed he is by my decision. My heart aches for him, and more than anything, I wish I didn't have to tell Jared good-bye. "As much as it hurts, I understand your choice. I love you and I love my brother. If you two want to work things out, then I'll step back. I won't stand in the way. I'll leave again, but I want you to know that I'll miss you every damn day for the rest of my life."

"This kills me. I don't want to end things like this," I tell him as my heart crumbles in my chest. "I've always loved you."

"But you love him too. I know you do or you wouldn't have married him. He was there for you when I wasn't." Tears run down Jared's cheeks. "Go tell him. You'll feel a lot better once everything is out in the open."

I nod, knowing that he's right. It was not good of me to tell Jared about the baby before Wes even had a chance to know. I need to tell him. "I should probably go find him."

Jared pulls me against him without apology and wraps his arms around me. "I love you, London. Forever."

"I love you so much." I cling to him, knowing this is probably the last time I'll ever feel his arms wrapped around me. "I don't want to let you go."

He cups my face and then swallows hard. "Sometimes the thing you love the most in this world is the one thing that you're destined to lose. I've come to learn in real life there are no happily ever afters." Jared's lips twist before he leans in and kisses my forehead.

I close my eyes and allow the tears I can no longer fight back to flow down my cheeks. I've been waiting for so long to have my Jared back—to feel his arms wrapped around me—and now that I finally have what I want, I have to set him free.

I pull away and dart out of the house, unable to stay with him one moment longer, because I know that if I stay locked in his embrace I'll talk myself out of doing the right thing and being with Wes.

A sob tears out of me as I run down the sidewalk and find the safety of my car. I lay my head on the steering wheel and allow myself to grieve the loss of the man I love, because I know this time it's really over.

After I've cried out every last tear, I pull out my cell phone and dial Wes's work number.

"Hey. It's me," I say after Wes answers. "I'm calling to ask if you would come over to the house for dinner tonight."

"Really? That would be amazing." The excitement in his voice is clear, and I can tell he's hopeful about what this invitation means. "What time?"

I force a smile on my face so that my voice doesn't sound sad. "Let's say six?"

"Sounds great. I'll see you then. I love you, London," he says.

"Love you too." I force the words out, and my heart sinks because it isn't ready for me to try and force it to love Wes.

This is the right thing to do. Wes is the father of my baby. He deserves a shot to be there for every moment in the child's life.

Later that day, I put on a blue sundress that Wes always compliments, saying how beautiful I look when I wear it, and then busy myself with making dinner while I wait on Wes to show up. I keep rehearsing how I'm going to break the news to him, but nothing I come up with ever sounds right. I guess there's not going to be any easy way to tell him any of this.

Wes doesn't even bother using the doorbell tonight. Instead he uses his house key to let himself inside. "London?"

I dry my hands off on a dish towel after washing off a tomato for the salad. "In here."

Wes walks in with his jacket in his hand while he loosens his tie. "Something smells good."

"I made homemade chicken and noodles," I tell him, knowing that's one of his favorites.

"Really? Wow. That's awesome. What's the special occasion? You usually only make those on holidays or my birthday. What's up?"

He's already suspicious. If I tell him now, we'll most likely end up in a fight and he won't eat, and I don't want to do that to him. "Sit. Let's eat."

I figure ignoring him the best I can is the right way to handle things for now.

I fix him a plate of food, carry it to the table, and set it down in front of him.

He tips his head forward and makes a show of taking a big whiff. "You are such an amazing cook."

I laugh as I make my plate and then join him at the small table in our kitchen. "I learned it all from your mom."

He grins. "I love that you're close with Mom. You always hear horror stories about wives hating their in-laws. I'm glad we don't have that problem."

I give him a closed-mouth smile. It's true, my mom would've probably loved Wes, but she would've loved Jared too. It would be nice to talk to her about both of them, because she could give me so much advice right now. It's not like I can go to Julie and seek out advice on which of her sons I should be with. She loves both of her boys. She doesn't want to see one of them hurt any more than I do.

The rest of the dinner we make small talk, and I listen intently as Wes tells me about a big project he's working on for his firm. I'm proud that he's accomplished so much since we've been out of school.

Wes downs the last bit of his drink and then focuses his attention directly on me. "Okay, now that we're done eating, are you going to tell me why you asked me to come here? I've been on pins and needles wondering what it could be since you called earlier today."

I chew on my bottom lip. "There are a couple things that I want to talk to you about."

"I'm all ears," he says.

I take a deep breath. "I've been feeling really sick over the last month, and I thought it was stress or maybe some sort of adult form of mono, but when I went to the doctor today, he told me it was something else."

He raises his eyebrows. "What is it?"

There's no simple way to say this, so I'm just going to blurt it out. "I'm pregnant."

Wes's jaw drops open for a split second before a huge grin overtakes his face. "A baby? I'm going to be a father? Oh, baby, that's such wonderful news." He reaches across the table and takes my hand. "This could be just what we need to get us back on track."

I lift one eyebrow. "You aren't upset that this has happened after all the plans we made to wait for a long while before we had kids?"

"I know we talked about that, but I just knew back when we first started having problems that maybe if we had a baby you'd be able to forget about my jackass brother and focus on the family you could have with me if you just got over him."

His words cause me to trip up a bit, and I rub my forehead as I replay what he just said in my mind. Wes has wanted a baby all along? "Wes, a baby doesn't save a marriage."

"Sure they do. Look at us. We're back to talking—working through things together." Wes smiles, and then his cheeks flush a bit. "I could see us falling apart, London. I would've done anything to keep you in my life. I didn't want to lose you to the ghost of my brother—a guy who I knew wasn't worthy of your love."

I flinch and shove myself away from the table before I pop right up out of my seat. "That's not for you to decide. My heart loves who it loves."

"London, come on. Don't get angry. This is a great thing for us. Look at this dinner you made—the baby is already bringing us closer together. Don't let the fact that Jared is in town for a little while mess with that, because, trust me, he's not planning on sticking around. As soon as that Ace White guy is found, Wicked White will go back on tour, and Jared will be going with them."

I furrow my brow. "Just because he leaves to go back out on the road doesn't mean that we wouldn't have been able to make a relationship work. We did it all the time when he was on the road playing baseball."

"That was short trips." Wes opens his mouth to say something else but just shakes his head instead and takes a deep breath. "London, I can't believe after all this time you're still sticking up for him. I'm so sick and tired of him always coming between us!"

I flinch at Wes's tone, and before I have a chance to say anything else, Wes fires at me, "What the two of you had is over. That night we tracked him down and saw him in the backseat with some random barfly . . . that was just a small taste of what life with Jared would be like for you. He didn't have the groupies back then like he does now. He's a rock star, and they're known for being wild and fucking everything that walks. Why would you want him back, knowing all that? I don't understand why you just can't let him go. He doesn't love you like I do. Can't you see that I would do anything for you?"

I open my mouth to argue that Jared has changed, but I know that it won't do any good. All Wes thinks about is the past. He's not willing to even give his brother the benefit of the doubt that he's figured out how to cope with his emotions.

Jared left me once and put me—all of us—through a lot, but I know when he apologized that he was sincere. More than anything, I want Jared and me to have a second chance at being together, but for my baby's sake, I can't. Wes is the right choice. He's safe, and he's what this baby needs: a stable father.

Wes shoves his hand into his hair and grimaces. "God, London. I can't believe you still love him after all he's put you through. Maybe when he finds out that you're carrying my baby, he'll finally figure out that he's lost. That you're mine."

I swallow hard as I stare into Wes's wild brown eyes. "Jared already knows about the baby."

"What? How the hell does he know?" Anger rings through his voice.

"I stopped by your mom's and he was there and I . . . well, I told him." I leave out all the details of our conversation—how I chose Wes over Jared because of the baby. There's no need to add even more insult to injury.

Wes flares his nostrils and tosses his napkin on the table. "Motherfucker!" He stands up and grabs his coat. "That's it. I've had it with him. I'm going to go over and put a stop to him ever contacting you again. You're *my* wife and"—he points to my belly—"that's *my* baby in there. *Mine.* Not his—*mine*—and I'm going to make sure he knows it."

Panic fills me. I don't want them fighting any more over me. I have to try and stop this before the whole situation spirals out of control.

"Wes . . . please don't—I'm sorry," I plead.

He shakes his head and licks the corner of his mouth, a move he always does when he's frustrated. "I'm done, London. Done. This ends tonight. I want him out of our lives forever. No more interference from him!"

He turns on his heel and walks out the door, not giving me a chance to say one more word. I know it's not fair that I told Jared about the baby first. It was wrong of me to do that, but at the time I felt like it was the right thing to do. I've played with Wes's heart for far too long, and by telling his brother about the baby first, it pushed him over the edge.

I start to chase after him, but he's too fast and he's already made it out to his car by the time I make it to the front door. When I open the door, Wes revs the engine of his blue Mustang and squeals the tires as he backs out onto the street.

I rush back into the kitchen to grab my keys. I know exactly where Wes is heading, and there's no way I want them to fight again over me. I have to stop this.

## NOW
## JARED

I stare at the beautiful Nova parked in the garage, and my thoughts instantly drift toward my father. He never did get to make it home to see how I got this thing up and running for him while he was gone. We worked on this car every spare moment we had together, other than the times he spent with me tossing a baseball or showing me how to play a guitar.

Dad was my hero. In my eyes he could do no wrong and was a superhero. I hope someday when I'm a father I can be half the man to my kid. Wes will be a good dad too. He's caring and smart, and I know he'll be around for the baby London's carrying no matter what, because that's the kind of guy he is. He's not some asshole like me who loses his mind and bails when things get tough. Doing something like that was never in Wes's blood. I didn't think it was in mine either until things got hard and I felt like I had no other choice but to leave in order to get my head straight. Now I'm trying like hell to make sure that I change that part of myself. I want to be the guy who's dependable.

The front door slams shut, and my back stiffens.

"Mom?" I call, but she doesn't answer, so I walk through the open garage door into the kitchen. I pause the moment my eyes land on Wes standing in the middle of the kitchen.

Wes rushes at me and grabs handfuls of my shirt. "You! I want you to stay the fuck away from London. She's *mine*. You got that?" he growls.

"I'm not going to fight you." I throw my hands up in the air. "She chose you, didn't she?!"

God that stings to admit out loud, but it's the truth. She made her choice to be with my brother—to start a family with him—and I have to respect that even though it kills me to know that I've lost her forever.

"I hate that she loves you—even after all this time." He shoves me backward into the fridge, and my heart thunders in my chest as I stare into my brother's wild brown eyes. "You got everything while I was overlooked! I always came in second compared to you. Do you know how much it hurt to know that Dad loved you more than me? If that wasn't enough, how about when the girl I've been in love with since elementary school falls for my younger, hotshot, baseball-playing brother? You had everything I always wanted, and you fucked it up like what you had meant nothing! When you walked out on this family, you didn't even bother to check and see how we were dealing with things because you were too wrapped up in your own grief to see that we were all hurting. Hell, you even turned your back on London, the one person who loves you more than anything else in this shit-hole world. She went through hell when you left, and I had to pick up all the pieces. I won't let you hurt London again."

His words sting because I never knew he felt like this. There's so much pent-up rage in him, and it's all directed at me. Wes is usually the calm one between us. It's hard to stand here and watch him fall apart like this, but I have to be honest with him.

"I won't apologize for loving her," I say. "But if you want to hit me, do it. I treated you like shit and I deserve your anger. So if you want to hit me, so be it, but it won't make me stop loving London. I'll always love her, even if she's with you."

"Ahhhhh!" Wes screams in my face as he draws his arm back, fist curled tight, ready to blast me.

"Do it!" My chest rises and falls as I await the pain that's sure to follow the blow as I give my brother permission to unleash his rage on me.

The next few seconds happen so fast. Wes's fist flies forward, and I squeeze my eyes shut, knowing I have this coming, knowing that deep down I deserve much worse than this. The force of his punch to my face causes my head to snap to the right. Warm blood fills my nose and then runs down over my top lip and drips to my mouth. The metallic taste fills my mouth, and I open my eyes just in time to witness Wes drawing his elbow back yet again.

I'm not angry with him—not at all—and I want him to know that. "I'm sorry."

Blow after blow, I don't try to fight any of them, and I apologize every time I get the chance. I welcome the pain. It's a reminder of how much I hurt everyone. Just as I'm about to lose consciousness, I hear an angelic voice scream my name. The voice rips through my foggy brain, and my eyes snap open just in time to see London rush through the kitchen and lunge after Wes just as he draws back yet again.

"London, stop!" I protest, but I can't get the words out fast enough.

As she leaps onto Wes's back, he draws his elbow back at the same time, landing it directly into her stomach. Instantly Wes realizes he's hit her on accident and releases me to turn around. Wes and

I both watch in horror as London grunts from the pain of the blow and drops to her knees. She releases a sob and instinctively wraps her arms around her stomach.

Wes drops to his knees beside her and attempts to comfort her. "Oh my God. London, are you all right? I'm so sorry. I didn't know you were there. Are you hurt?"

I slide down the wall, barely able to see out of the one eye that isn't swollen shut, and watch as panic engulfs my brother.

London sits there on the floor, crying so hard that she can barely catch her breath. Every muscle in her body shakes violently as she lifts her chin to lock her gaze with Wes's. "What were you thinking? Look at his face!" she shouts before she sucks in a ragged breath. "Look at what you've done to him, Wes!"

My heart squeezes in my chest when I hear her defend me. I wish I could thank her—hold her—comfort her, but I know that would only make things worse with Wes, so I sit there, quiet.

Wes walks over to London and stretches out his hand. "I lost it. I'm sorry. Come back home with me."

The word "home" might as well be another punch in the gut. The thought of him taking her home and being the one to comfort her hurts so fucking bad.

Tears stream down London's face as she takes his hand and allows him to help her up. The sight of them together is almost more than I can take. When he pulls her in against his chest, I drop my eyes down to the floor by their feet so I don't have to watch this tender moment take place right in front of me.

It's then I notice blood trickling down London's legs, just above her knees. Oh my God. She's hurt. Energy surges through me and I shove myself up from the floor to stand on my own two feet. "London? Are you all right?" Her beautiful green eyes point in my direction, and I motion down to her legs. "You're bleeding."

"Oh, God. No!" is all she manages to say before Wes and I look at each other with wide eyes as the realization of what's happening to her hits us.

"Come on. I'll drive us to the hospital," I say and grab the keys to my rental off the counter.

Wes leads London out the door but doesn't once fight me on being the one driving them. The entire fifteen-minute ride over to the hospital, Wes apologizes to London, blaming himself for what's happening to her.

I can empathize with the agony he feels. Five years ago, I was the one who lost control and hurt London, which was how I knew I was no longer the right guy for her. I allowed my own pain and anger to blind me to the point where I physically lashed out at others.

It's hard for me to know that I'm the source of my brother's rage, and more than anything I wish he knew how truly sorry I am for hurting him all those times in the past.

The tile below my feet is worn from the high traffic that comes in and out of the emergency room. I pace while I wait to hear how London's doing. She's been back there nearly an hour, and I've received no word.

I look up just in time to see Mom walking toward me with a worried expression on her face. She cradles my face in her hands as she examines me. "Wes did this? Are you sure you don't need to see a doctor too while we're here?"

I pull her hands down, away from my face. "I'll be fine, Mom. Nothing a little time and ice won't heal. I'm more concerned with London right now."

"How is she?" Mom asks.

I shake my head. "I don't know. Wes hasn't come out to tell me anything."

"Mom?" I turn around when I hear Wes call for our mother. "She's asking for you."

Mom pats my arm. "Don't worry, honey. I'm sure she's going to be okay."

I nod as she takes off back through the double wooden doors with Wes. Needing some fresh air, I make my way outside of the building and find a quiet bench to sit on. I rest my elbows on my thighs and allow my head to drop down while I say a little silent prayer that London will be okay.

"Do you mind if I sit?" I look up to see Wes standing there with his hands shoved deep in his front pockets.

I scoot over. "Sure . . . unless you want to hit me some more."

I'm only half kidding, because I don't think I'll be able to take many more punches to the face.

After a couple seconds of debate, Wes sits down. "You don't know how bad I wish I could hit you, but for some crazy reason I can't make myself do it. You are still my brother, and other than Mom, you're the only family that I have left. I won't hurt you, no matter how I much hate you right now. I know we both care for London, and right now she needs us both to be strong for her. She lost the baby."

Tears form in my eyes. "I'm so sorry, Wes."

Wes is more of a man than me. When I was angry, I forgot all about the strong bond of family, and it took me five years to man up and face the people who I pointed all my anger on, Wes included. I took my anger out on him—he became the target of my rage because he was one of the people who was closest to me. Family is the most important thing in this world. We need to figure out a way to heal all the wounds in ours and find a way to move forward.

"I'm sorry, Wes. I've apologized to London, but I need you to hear it too. I know that I was wrong to leave the way I did. All I can do is ask for your forgiveness."

"How can I forgive you when you return home after five years to the person I love most in the world, and she wants you more than she wants me? Do you know how much that kills me?" he says.

I can tell that he's hurting, but I am too. "The same way I can forgive you for moving in on the one woman I've loved since I was just a kid while I was gone."

He raises his eyebrows in surprise as he thinks about what I've said. "I always hated that she picked you over me. She never even looked in my direction until you were gone. I was her consolation prize—the next-best thing to you that she could find. I know that she still loves you. She made that very clear to me over the years, and I hate that. I hate that she couldn't move on past you and see that I loved her too. We both want her, and I don't know how to fix this, because no matter who she chooses, someone's getting hurt."

I frown as I think back to the first time London traipsed into our yard to play baseball with Wes and me. We both did our best to impress her—to win her over—so we've been fighting over her for so long, but only she gets to decide who wins. "It's not up to us. It never has been. It's always been her choice."

That gets me thinking about how things are different now that there's no baby. London made it clear to me that the reason she was picking Wes was because she was pregnant and wanted Wes in the baby's life. I would've never stood in the way of that if that's what London really wanted, but now I see a glimmer of hope that we may be able to get back together.

Wes rakes his fingers through his blond hair. "As much as I hate to admit it, I know you're right. I know she still loves you. I've been fighting hard to get her to see that I'm a better choice for her than you, but I can see it when I look in her eyes that her heart still belongs to you. That doesn't stop me from loving her and praying that even though you're back, that it's me that she chooses."

I stare at my brother, and I can completely relate to what he's feeling, but it still doesn't mean that I will just step aside and let London go without a fight. I know she'll need time to heal after all this, and time is one thing that I have on my hands right now.

"I can understand that," I say. "But before I leave this town again, I will make damn sure that she knows how much I love her and pray that she'll give me another shot with her heart."

Wes shakes his head. "And what if she doesn't want to be with you? She could just as easily pick me."

"If she does choose you, I'll leave again—this time for good. I don't want to stand in the way of you and London working things out if that's what she wants." The idea of never seeing London again is something I don't even want to consider. There wasn't a day that passed over the five years that I was gone that I didn't think of her—dream about what it would be like to hold her again—and now that I've had her again, it's going to be unbelievably difficult to walk away a second time. But it's what needs to happen if she chooses Wes, and I want him to know that I'll understand if she does decide to be with him.

I sigh and look my brother square in the eye. "You, London, and Mom are my family, and more than anything else, I want you to be happy."

"What about you?" he asks. "If she picks me, where does that leave you?"

"Alone—but I'll always have my music to keep me company." I muster up a smile so he can't tell that there's a breaking heart inside my chest.

Before he has time to say anything else, Wes's cell phone rings. "London?" He holds up his hand, palm out like he's trying to show her the sign to stop through the phone, but it's like London is in full-on panic mode on the other end of the line. "Slow down." He pauses again. "I'm on my way."

I stand there, watching—hoping he'll fill me in.

He glances up at me, and tears glisten in his eyes. "I have to go. London wants me in there."

I nod but don't say anything else before he turns and walks back inside the building.

After they release London from the hospital, I drive back to Mom's place. My mind is still going ninety miles an hour as I think about London and my family. More than anything I want to hop in the car and drive over to London's house to check on her, but I know Wes is there, and the two of them need time to grieve over what they've lost. I know he'll take good care of her, so I'm not worried about that, but it doesn't change the fact that I wish I was the one there for her.

Thinking about their loss makes me think of Dad, and I go to the garage.

Mom asked me when I got here a couple days ago if I'd been to his grave, and I told her no. That's not the place I feel closest to him. His gravestone is just a rock, a place where his body rests. It's not where I feel his spirit. I feel it in the music I play and in all the things we did together. That's when I can close my eyes and imagine his hand patting me on the shoulder.

Sitting here in this Nova, I sense that connection more than ever. It's the one place where I feel him the most.

I ran from the pain of losing him, but more than anything, I ran from the very memory of him. When I found out I lost him, everything in my life fell apart. Nothing made sense anymore because without him I couldn't see the path to my future clearly. That's why I had to leave this town and everyone in it behind. Everywhere I looked, I was reminded of Dad, and that brought more pain on me than I could handle.

It took me a while to accept that he was really gone—even longer to realize that the connection I shared with my father exists whether he's alive or dead because he still lives inside me. Inside this car, the bittersweet joy of feeling him now hits me hard.

"Hi, Dad," I whisper as I run my hand over the dash while sitting in the passenger seat.

Stirring up the dust on the dash causes me to sneeze, and my knees jerk up and hit the glove box. When it falls open, I furrow my brow when I spot a few white envelopes in there.

I don't remember these ever being in there.

I pick one of the sealed envelopes up and read my name etched across the front in Dad's thick scrawl. My hands shake as I realize this is some kind of letter addressed to me—a letter that holds the last conversation I'll ever technically have with my father.

I press the letter against my chest and close my eyes. Part of me thinks I should never open this letter, but keep it intact so that I will always have a piece of him to look forward to, while another part of me aches to find out what he could've possibly written to me about.

With a shaky hand, I carefully open the envelope, taking care to not rip the letter that's inside.

My eyes zero in on the words on the paper, and I take my time reading them. I want to absorb every second of it, because it's almost as if Dad's speaking to me one last time.

*Jared,*

*You might be wondering why in the hell I wrote letters and stuck them inside this car. Well, first thing is, I left them here because I figured no one would come across them in the glove box unless I've died, and, well, if that's how you found them, let me start off by telling you that I'm sorry.*

*Saying sorry hasn't always come easy for me—learning to admit when I'm wrong took a lot of practice. I wish I could say that I've always been the man you've come to know as you grew up, but the truth is, in my younger days I could be a hotheaded bastard. Lucky for me, your mom came along and helped straighten me out. She was there for me even when I didn't want her to be.*

*I hope that you can find the kind of love someday that I shared with your mother. By the looks of things from where I sit, I think you might already have with London. That girl is something, Jared, and I can tell that she's really in love with you. Hang on to that with both hands, because finding someone in this world who will love you despite all your flaws is a rarity, and you should cherish it.*

*The second thing I want to tell you is that I love you, and if, God forbid, I don't make it home to tell you this myself, I'm so very proud of the man that you've become. You are so strong and have talent coming out of your pores. Anything you've ever set your mind to doing, you've always succeeded at, and I admire that.*

*I want you to know if I'm on the other side, I'm watching over you, and I'll be around to give you a swift angel-style ass kickin' if you get out of line, so be good.*

*Well, that's about all I can think of—you know how I hate writing letters. Make sure you take care of your mother for me. If I'm gone, she's going to need you. Same goes for your brother. I know he's older than you, but he looks up to you.*

*Oh, and would you mind giving your mom and Wes their letters if I am gone? I would appreciate it. But, if you've found this and I'm still away, just put them in a place where no one else will find them.*

*Love,*
*Dad*

Tears stream down my face as I read the letter over and over. I can practically hear his voice in my head as I read the words. This is exactly how he would've spoken to me had he been here. I cradle the letter to my chest and finally release all the built-up tears I've been holding back for my father.

## NOW
## LONDON

It's been a month since I lost the baby. The first few days after it happened, I didn't even want to get out of bed. It's been so hard to keep it together, because every time I think about the little life I lost before I even fully had a chance to accept that I was pregnant to begin with, I can't stop the tears from flowing down my cheeks. Sam's been around a lot, motivating me to get up and keep living my life. I don't know what I would've done if she hadn't been here for me.

Jared called more times than I can count, begging to come see me, but I told him that I just wasn't ready to deal with things between us right now, that I needed some time to myself, so he's recently settled for texting me once a day. Losing the baby, ending my marriage for good—it all took a toll on me, and I didn't think I could handle hearing Jared reject me too if he decided he could no longer be with me.

Julie stops in quite a bit too, and I'm grateful for that. She knows everything that's been going on with me and both of her sons and hasn't once said one cross word to me about the situation.

Wes was devastated over the loss. When we were in the emergency room, he sat by my side and held my hand while we both cried together after the doctor told us that the baby was gone. Hearing that news—it's not something I'd wish on my worst enemy, because that was the worst day of my life.

Wes and I haven't talked much since then. When he came home with me to care for me after the miscarriage, he begged me to work things out with him—to not go through with the divorce—but I told him I just didn't love him the way he deserved. After that, I think he finally came to terms with my decision. He called to check on me a few times, but after he was sure that I was all right, he began contacting me less.

For the last week and a half I haven't heard at all from him, so I can't say that I'm shocked to be sitting here staring at a stack of dissolution papers that I just received from Wes's attorney. I'm not sad like I thought I would be when this day finally came. It's more of a relief to know that things are officially over between us—that Wes is in agreement that we can never make this marriage work.

Peyton and Brody busy themselves playing with a few toys that Sam brought over with them while I nervously pick at my fingernails. Sam's been over nearly every day since school let out two weeks ago, and it's been nice having her and the boys here so I don't have to be alone.

Sam sets her coffee mug onto the table at the end of my couch. "London, have you decided if you're going to go see Jared before he goes back on tour now that they've found Wicked White's front man? I mean, that's no secret that you're still hung up on him."

I shrug. "I've been trying to create some space between me and the Kraft boys. I don't know if I should go talk to him. It feels too soon to run from Wes to Jared since the baby and everything."

"You've been through a lot, and I'm sure Jared doesn't want to push you to be with him until you're ready, so he'll wait. I have a feeling that guy isn't going anywhere," Sam says.

The phone rings, and my head snaps. "What if it's Wes checking to see if I got these papers? I don't know if I'm ready to talk to him just yet."

Sam sighs while the phone continues to ring, but I don't dare check the caller ID. "London, you love Jared. It's no secret. We all know it. Wes knows it too. If you and Jared decide to get back together, it won't shock anyone, especially not Wes. It's time you finally make a decision about who you want to be with. I don't want to see you go back to that sad sack who is still hung up on a man from the past. Either be with Jared or move on."

I sigh. She's right. My life is at a crossroads, and I need to pick a path to move forward on.

I reach over and pick the phone up. "Hello?"

"London, can I come over? We need to talk." Jared's voice makes me sit up a little straighter because it's like a sign of fate.

I lick my lips slowly and then take a deep breath. I have the feeling my future is about to be given a clear path. "Okay. I'll be here."

The sound of car keys jingling in the background catches my attention before he says, "I'm on my way, then. See you in twenty minutes."

He gives no further explanation as to what's so urgent that he needs to come over here right away, and my mind goes crazy playing a million different scenarios of what's about to go down.

Sam stares at me. "Wes?"

I shake my head as I set the phone back down, still wondering what's going to happen when he gets here. "No, actually, that was Jared. He said we need to talk and he'll be here soon."

She raises her eyebrows. "Then that's my cue to load up my heathens and split."

When she stands, I wrap my arms around her and bury my face in her hair. "Thank you for being such an amazing friend to me. You always know just the right things to say."

She pulls back and smiles. "Anytime. What are best friends for?"

Twenty minutes later there's a knock on my door. I rush over, and the moment I open the door and see Jared, a rush of butterflies flutters in the pit of my stomach.

My eyes flit over his face, and I'm curious as to why he's standing on my doorstep after us not having much contact other than his daily texts. "Is everything all right?"

Jared nods and then gives me a sad smile. "It's fine. Can I come in?"

I push open the door. "Of course."

Jared steps up and wraps me in a one-armed hug once he's inside the door, but he seems so hesitant, like he's trying to respect me and not overstep some boundary with me. "I've missed you."

I squeeze him back, but his tone worries me, and I know he's probably here to tell me good-bye. "I've missed you too."

I walk into the living room and sit in the chair and motion to the couch, where I offer Jared a seat.

Jared clears his throat. "I know you said you needed space, and I don't want to push you to talk to me before you are ready, but I needed to come here to tell you good-bye."

My heart clenches because I knew this day was quickly closing in on us. I'm not ready for him to go yet. I don't want to lose him again, but I can't force him to stay and be with me. I've been keeping up with reports on his band while I've been at home. Every channel on TV has been running the story about the missing Wicked White front man.

"I heard they found Ace White," I say.

He nods. "They found him in some dumpy trailer park in Ohio. The guy didn't want to be found, that's for sure." He sighs. "I talked with my tour manager, Jane Ann, and she told me it was best if I come back to California, because as soon as Ace gets back, the label wants to throw us into the studio. They want to cash in on all this publicity, since Ace's disappearance thrust the band into the limelight."

"So are you leaving now . . . or tomorrow?" Selfishly I wish that the answer will be never, since I want more time with him so we can figure out whatever this thing is between us.

"My flight is tomorrow evening, but that's what I've come to talk to you about."

I lift my eyebrows. "Oh?"

"I want you to come with me." My eyes widen, but he holds up his hand, palm out. "I know that sounds crazy, but just hear me out. You're out on summer break, and I figured if you came with me, we'd have a couple weeks to spend together—just the two of us—at my place, getting to know each other again."

"You still want to be with me—even after everything?" I ask.

Jared nods. "I know things are still raw, but I want you to know that I need you in my life. If you're ready to move on, I want it to be with me. I've already explained my intentions to my brother. He knows that I still love you." Jared reaches over and takes my hand in his. "I guess what I'm asking is if you're willing to give me another chance at your heart."

My heart thumps hard in my chest. This is what I've been waiting on for five years. I've missed him and what we had together so much.

"If you give me another shot, I swear I'll do right by you. I'll guard your heart every second of every day, and I promise I will never let you down again. You can count on me, London. I'm a changed man," he pleads.

Jared's eyebrows pull in, and a slight frown flickers across his face when I don't immediately answer. This is a huge, life-changing decision, but when I stare into his eyes I see sincerity in them. He's proved since he showed back up in my life that he's changed—that he's in control and has a better ability to deal with adversity and pain. He's matured, and he's become a man I can picture spending the rest of my life with.

The concern in his eyes chokes me up a bit. I'm sure waiting for my decision isn't easy on him, but after what he put me through, he deserves to sweat it out while I make up my mind.

I stare at him, and a tear slips down my cheek. Jared is quickly by my side. The way he wraps his arms around me, pulling me in tight, makes me feel like he's willing to be there to protect me for-ever. I cry harder as I worry that one day, just like Wes said, Jared will leave me behind again to go be some rock star, and I'll be left here alone.

"Don't cry," he whispers and folds me into his arms even tighter. "I've got you."

I cling to him like he's my life raft on a sinking ship. "Prom-ise me that I won't lose you again, Jared, because you're all I've got. I won't make it through us splitting up again if I let you back into my heart."

His fingers smooth down the hair on the back of my head. "You don't have to worry about that, London. I won't leave your side again. I swear it to you, and I mean that."

"Please don't ever break that vow," I say as I burrow myself against him.

Jared pulls back and cradles my face in both of his hands. "I swear it. I'll be here for you until I take my last breath on this earth. I've learned my lesson about staying away from you. You are every-thing to me, London. I know I have a crazy way of showing it, but you are and always have been. I spent five long years without you, and I know that being away from you is something I never want to go through again. You make me a better man, and no matter what life throws at us, I'll stick by your side and keep my fucking temper in check because I never want to do anything that fucks this up," he whispers.

He pulls me in for a simple kiss. "I love you, London, and nothing on this earth will ever change that."

I take a deep breath and close my eyes. The look in his blue eyes tells me he means every word of what he's saying, so the best thing is to tell him how I feel in return. "I love you too, and I'll come with you to California."

"I think I could get used to hearing that again every day," he murmurs against my lips before I fade into his kiss.

## TWO YEARS LATER
## LONDON

Standing side stage watching one of the hottest rock bands perform is truly an amazing experience, and I never grow tired of it. I watch in awe as my man is in his element, entertaining thousands of people with his phenomenal skill. Jared Kraft was made to be center stage.

Ace, the lead singer of the band, steps up to the microphone and thanks the crowd for coming out to see them. It's been amazing to see the transformation of this band. They've really become a cohesive unit. They are nothing like the band I first met a couple years ago. Ace and Jared hated one another back then. According to Jared, they both went through a bit of a transformation during the break Ace took from being a rock star, both of them finding love and being humbled.

"Hey, London," Tyler says as he passes me with Luke by his side, who gives me a simple wave.

Finally Jared makes his way off stage and then carefully wraps his arms around me. "What are you doing up here? The doctor said no strenuous activity. It's not good for the baby." He reaches down and rubs my round belly, which is holding his daughter, and smiles when she kicks. "She's active today."

I place my hand on my stomach. "I think she likes the music."

His eyes widen and he bends down at the waist to talk to my belly. "You're far too young to be a rocker chick, young lady."

I laugh and roll my eyes as he hooks my arm with his. When we make it to the tour bus, I spot Iris, Ace's brown-haired girlfriend, sitting on the steps of the bus while she watches her two-and-a-half-year-old toss rocks in the parking lot.

It's funny how becoming a father and a soon-to-be-father has chilled both Ace and Jared out. It's done wonders for the band since these two have learned to coexist and not fly off the handle at one another every chance they get. Jared no longer seems obsessed with taking over as front man anymore either. He told me since I've come back into his life, he's been too preoccupied with me to worry about the dynamics of the band as much.

Ace's son, AJ, looks up and notices Jared and me coming in his direction and runs to us with his arms spread wide. "Wondon!"

I bend down to pick him up, but Jared beats me to it and scoops him up. Jared looks at me and shakes his finger side to side. "No heavy lifting either, remember?"

"AJ weighs all of twenty pounds. I think I would've been fine," I scold him, but secretly it makes me so happy that he's such a protective father. He's already so amazing with AJ, so he's getting his practice in for when our baby comes.

"Dadda?" AJ asks Jared.

"In two minutes, buddy. He's busy talking to reporter people." Jared holds up two fingers. "Can you say two?"

"Doooo," AJ repeats, and we all clap like it's the greatest thing ever.

I watch Jared with AJ, and I swear if I weren't already pregnant, I would be from just watching him with Iris and Ace's son.

"He's so adorable," I tell Iris.

Iris smiles, causing her teeth to sparkle. No wonder the girl is a famous Broadway star. I bet people pay money to just stare at her. And to top it all off, she's supersweet. I can see why Ace is so gaga over her.

"Tired, Momee," AJ says to Iris, monopolizing all of her attention.

Iris stretches her arms out to AJ, and Jared hands him over to her.

Jared smiles as AJ yawns and stretches his chubby little arms. "Looks like this one is all partied out."

"Make that two—I'm beat myself," Iris says. "I think I'll go inside and put us both to bed."

"See you later," I say before she waves and heads inside the bus.

When we're alone, Jared wraps me in his arms and places a sweet little peck on my lips. "I can't wait until our kid gets here. You'll be such an awesome mom."

I smile at him. "And you'll be a great father."

I'm still grinning like an idiot as he holds me in his arms. Suddenly I realize that this moment in my life is perfect. I've gotten everything that I've ever wanted: I've married the man who I've loved since middle school. Wes has moved on and is now dating a rambunctious bartender named Rhonda, and from what I hear is getting pretty serious with her. Julie and my dad are both over-the-moon excited to meet their soon-to-be-born grandchild, and it's funny to watch them argue over what we should name our kid when we get together once a month for a family dinner.

It was a long road to get to this point, but I'm glad we finally made it here, and I can't wait to spend the rest of my life with Jared.

# ACKNOWLEDGMENTS

First off, I want to thank you, my dear readers, for giving this book a shot!

Emily Snow, thank you for being there for me over the years. Your input on my books has been a lifesaver.

Jennifer Wolfel, I can never thank you enough for reading a million versions of this story and hashing out the bugs with me and not allowing me to give up on Jared and London.

Toski Covey, thank you for being my first test subject on this story idea. I can't tell you how much I appreciate our little chats about this story line.

Jennifer Foor, thank you for being amazing and sharing your killer writing methods with me!

Holly Malgieri, thank you for reading the very first draft of this book and giving me feedback!

Jill Marsal, thank you for being an amazing agent!

Charlotte Herscher, thank you for working so hard on this book! Your input made it so much better!

To my amazing team at Montlake, you guys are wicked awesome!

My beautiful ladies in Valentine's Vixens Group, you all are the best. You guys always brighten my day and push me to be a better writer. Thank you!

To the romance blogging community, thank you for always supporting me and my books. I can't tell you how much every share, tweet, post, and comment means to me. I read them all, and every time I feel giddy. Thank you for everything you do. Blogging is not an easy job, and I can't tell you how much I appreciate what you do for indie authors like me. You totally make our world go round.

Last, but always first in my life, my husband and son: thank you for putting up with me. I love you both more than words can express.

# ABOUT THE AUTHOR

Michelle A. Valentine is the *New York Times* and *USA Today* bestselling author of *Rock the Heart*. *Wicked Reunion* is the second novel in her Wicked White romance series. She attended college as a drafting and design major, but her love of people soon persuaded her to join the nursing field. It wasn't until after the birth of her son that she began her love affair with romance novels, and she hasn't looked back since. When she's not writing, she feeds her music addiction, dabbles in party planning, and expresses herself by working with arts and crafts. She currently lives in Columbus, Ohio, with her husband, son, and two beloved dogs.

14161713R00132

Printed in Great Britain
by Amazon.co.uk, Ltd.,
Marston Gate.